THE SCION

PREVIOUS BOOKS BY ALAN REFKIN

FICTION

Matt Moretti and Han Li Series

The Archivist
The Abductions
The Payback

Mauro Bruno Detective Series

The Patriarch
The Artifact

NONFICTION

The Wild Wild East: Lessons for Success in Business in Contemporary Capitalist China
Alan Refkin and Daniel Borgia, PhD

Doing the China Tango: How to Dance around Common Pitfalls in Chinese Business Relationships
Alan Refkin and Scott Cray

Conducting Business in the Land of the Dragon: What Every Businessperson Needs to Know about China
Alan Refkin and Scott Cray

Piercing the Great Wall of Corporate China: How to Perform Forensic Due Diligence on Chinese Companies
Alan Refkin and David Dodge

THE SCION

BOOK 2 OF THE MAURO BRUNO DETECTIVE SERIES

ALAN REFKIN

THE SCION
BOOK 2 OF THE MAURO BRUNO DETECTIVE SERIES

iUniverse books may be ordered through booksellers or by contacting:

iUniverse
1663 Liberty Drive
Bloomington, IN 47403
www.iuniverse.com
1-800-Authors (1-800-288-4677)

ISBN: 978-1-5320-9909-0 (sc)
ISBN: 978-1-5320-9910-6 (e)

Library of Congress Control Number: 2020907078

Print information available on the last page.

iUniverse rev. date: 04/21/2020

To my wife, Kerry
To Ann Margaret Refkin

CHAPTER 1

MAURO BRUNO WATCHED Elia Donati doing the perp walk out the front entrance of the Ritz Hotel in Paris. Wearing a robe and slippers, and with his hands cuffed behind his back, the chief inspector showed no emotion as he was led toward the waiting police vehicle. It was late afternoon in the City of Lights as the well-heeled guests of the most famous hotel in the world stopped to watch the handsome six-foot-tall man in his midthirties being led past them, flanked by two uniformed officers. Bruno, who was dressed in the same attire as the perp, watched the officers carefully place his friend into the back seat of the police cruiser. A few moments later, with the blue lights atop the police cruiser flashing, the vehicle parted the dense traffic on the Place Vendôme and left the area.

"Perhaps we can go to your room, and you can tell me again how you and Chief Inspector Donati discovered the body," said Capitaine Luc Guimond of the Paris police, pointing to the revolving door of the hotel.

The five-foot-ten French detective, who had a neatly trimmed beard and mustache and black hair that was curved back in a defined wave, giving him a confident look, followed Bruno into the hotel, up the stairs to the right of the entrance,

1

and down the first-floor hall. The detective was in his early thirties and was considered by his peers to be both unusually smart and a workaholic, a fact evidenced by his rapid rise to the rank of capitaine, which was generally earned by those with a decade more of experience. Bruno, with the rank of chief inspector in Italy's Polizia di Stato, was rank-equivalent to Guimond.

The chief inspector had already told his story to his French counterpart. The fact the Guimond wanted to hear it again didn't surprise him because police procedures at this stage of an investigation were pretty much the same: look for inconsistencies and changes in someone's story. The fact that Bruno had given up smoking, going from nearly three packs a day to zero, didn't help his mood. It was the hardest thing he'd ever done, physically and emotionally. But after attending his father's funeral, he had realized that if he didn't quit, he'd cut decades from his life—not to mention eventually having the lung capacity of a hummingbird.

After they entered Bruno's room, Guimond removed a small digital recorder from his pocket and placed it on the desk. He then directed Bruno to take a seat in the brown leather club chair to the side of the window while he went to the straight-backed wooden chair in front of the desk, pulled it out, and placed it close to the chief inspector.

"Please start at the beginning," Guimond said, turning on the recorder.

Bruno, who stood five feet eleven and was a good ten pounds overweight, leaned back in his chair. He had salt-and-pepper hair combed straight back, a neatly trimmed black mustache with flecks of gray, and piercing brown eyes. He spoke passable French, at least enough to understand and respond to Guimond. After taking a deep breath to calm himself, he began to repeat the story that he'd given the detective earlier.

"My flight from Venice arrived at Charles de Gaulle Airport at noon. I took a taxi directly from there to the hotel, arriving at approximately one," Bruno said. "I then went to the registration desk, where I filled out the required guest information and presented my passport for inspection. I was then escorted to my room by one of the hotel staff."

"You and the accused are both chief inspectors with the Italian Polizia di Stato?"

"Yes, but as I said, Chief Inspector Donati works in Milan, and I in Venice. We're here to celebrate my birthday and his promotion to chief inspector."

"They must pay well in Italy for you both to afford this hotel."

"We probably have comparable pay scales to your police force, Capitaine, so this hotel is not remotely affordable. Fortunately, Chief Inspector Donati is from a very wealthy family. They have a decades-old tradition of spending the week between Christmas and New Year at the Ritz Paris. Somehow that seems to have resulted in Chief Inspector Donati being given two rooms gratis for a week."

"How long ago was that?"

"As I said earlier, he received the invitation for this stay fifteen days ago. Coincidentally, the timing was perfect, since the date of the stay coincided with celebratory events in both of our lives, which is why he invited me."

"Just as you told me earlier," Guimond said. "However, when I checked with the hotel, they said that both your rooms, as well as additional money for expenses, had been prepaid by an anonymous person using an offshore account. Someone who is very wealthy must like the both of you to put twenty-five thousand euros toward your hotel stay. Or do you think a better explanation is that they're repaying a past favor? Perhaps you and Chief Inspector Donati have another source of income?"

Bruno bit the inside of his cheek to prevent himself from saying something that he'd regret. This restraint didn't go unnoticed by Guimond. A few seconds later, Bruno relaxed his jaw muscles.

"Since I'm hearing this information for the first time, all I can say is that neither Chief Inspector Donati nor I knew that fact when we received the invitation. Otherwise, we wouldn't have come."

"You didn't call the hotel to confirm the gratis rates, as you put it?"

"Chief Inspector Donati told me that he called and confirmed that the rooms were at no charge to us. The only stipulation was that we had to begin our stay within fifteen days."

"Continue—you were saying that a staff member escorted you to your room."

"After the person escorting me to my room left, I unpacked. I then changed into my swimming trunks, robe, and slippers and phoned Chief Inspector Donati, who was in the adjoining room. He had texted me earlier that he'd made an appointment for each of us to have a massage, after which we'd avail ourselves of the pool and the bar next to it." Bruno reached into his robe pocket and grabbed his iPhone. He pulled up his messages and handed the device to Guimond, who looked at the screen before returning the phone.

"Did either of you request these specific rooms?"

This was a new question that Guimond had not asked in his previous interrogation. The response Bruno was about to give wouldn't help Donati one bit. However, he understood that Guimond probably knew the truth and was testing his truthfulness.

"I believe the chief inspector requested these rooms when he spoke to the reservation department to set our arrival date. He told me that we'd be staying in the exact rooms that he and his parents occupy during their stays. They apparently like this wing of the hotel because it offers convenient access to the bars, restaurants, and spa."

"What happened next?"

"As we were walking down the hall to take the elevator to the spa, we both heard a scream coming from the last room on the right."

"Room 102."

"I didn't see the room number. The door was open, and when we entered, we saw the housekeeper standing over the body of a well-dressed man. I checked his pulse, but there was none."

"Where was Chief Inspector Donati when you did this?"

"He was standing beside me the entire time," Bruno said, again repeating the answer he'd given earlier. He said this without changing the cadence of his response or the inflection in his voice, even though what he was telling Guimond was a lie. Donati had begun searching the room and found photos of himself and Bruno on the desk. He had also discovered, when looking through a nylon bag, seemingly the sole luggage brought by the victim, bank statements from an offshore bank that showed that Bruno and Donati each had $1 million in accounts there—which was news to them. Bruno had folded the statements and photos and placed them in his robe pocket before the police arrived. Upon returning to his room, he had placed both the photos and the statements in a plastic bag and hidden them under the artificial begonias in the flower box on his balcony. He needed time to investigate before this case went nuclear, which wasn't going to happen if Guimond took possession of what they'd found.

"And a few minutes later, the police arrived," Guimond said.

"Accompanied by the hotel manager and the housekeeper," Bruno added. "Five minutes later, you and a number of others began to arrive. After you took my statement, I returned to my room."

"You and Inspector Donati went to your rooms together?"

"Yes."

"Perhaps to get your stories straight?"

"At that point, we'd already given our statements to you."

"True," Guimond conceded.

"I have a question, Capitaine," Bruno said.

Guimond nodded, indicating that Bruno could ask.

"Who's the dead man?"

"I'm glad you asked. The victim's name is Alberto Abate, and five months ago, he was arrested by Chief Inspector Donati for possession of thirty kilos of heroin. However, not long after, it was stolen from impound, thereby necessitating that all charges against Abate be dropped."

Bruno was momentarily stunned and didn't respond to what he had been told. If what the French detective said was true, and he had every reason to believe it was, then why hadn't Donati told him about Abate?

"I heard about the theft," Bruno finally said in response.

"I'm sure you and every police officer in Italy did. The officer on duty at the impound facility and two of his fellow officers were killed in the theft. The drugs were never recovered—until now."

"They were found?"

"Not more than an hour ago in Milan. They were in the trunk of a black two-door BMW 528i coupe."

Bruno didn't have to ask who the BMW belonged to. He had been in Donati's car.

"I'm sure you're familiar with Chief Inspector Donati's vehicle. It appears that he and Monsieur Abate had a business relationship, which the chief inspector decided to terminate."

Bruno began to question how well he knew Donati. He had thought he'd had him pegged after the chief inspector saved his life on more than one occasion. Still, what Guimond had just told him was extremely suspicious. The fact that Donati knew the victim and hadn't said anything to Bruno about it, the fact that the murder weapon was his, the fact that the missing drugs were discovered in his car, the fact that the victim was staying down the hall from them, and the fact that their hotel stay was said to be gratis was just too much for anyone, much less a police detective, to accept as coincidence.

"I'm not sure that assumption is correct," Bruno said, responding to Guimond's statement. "All you have is circumstantial evidence."

"Since the murder weapon belongs to Chief Inspector Donati, and his prints are on the weapon," Guimond responded, showing Bruno a text that he'd just received confirming the prints, "I believe I have more than circumstantial evidence."

"And being his friend automatically makes me a suspect," Bruno said, saying what he believed Guimond was already thinking.

"It explains how you both had the resources to afford this hotel, why the money was wired from an overseas account, and the stupid story that you both concocted to justify your stay. Let me tell you how this will play out, although I'm sure you already know the drill—the first one to tell the truth and give up his partner gets the deal. Confess, tell me what you know, and you won't spend the rest of your life in prison."

"The deal you've just offered me only works if we're guilty. You've spent, what, all of four hours investigating this case? I want to believe that the reason you climbed the police department ranks so quickly is that you were smarter than your colleagues and solved crimes that seemed unsolvable, not that you tried to intimidate people into pleading guilty before you determined the truth. I'm innocent. Chief Inspector Donati is innocent. And the faster you get off your ass and really investigate what's going on, the quicker you'll arrive at that truth." Bruno was mad, and his voice reflected his rapidly increasing blood pressure.

"Then you don't know the deceased, nor do you have any knowledge of the drugs, the gun, the offshore account, or who paid for this room?"

"What I know is that my friend is innocent and that he's not stupid. How convenient that the murder weapon, which happened to have the chief inspector's prints on it because the gun belonged to him before it was stolen, was hidden beneath the victim. How convenient that the stolen drugs were found in the trunk of his car. And how convenient that a man he once arrested was staying at this hotel and down the hall from his room. Nothing is ever this neat in a homicide— you know that."

"Normally, I'd agree with you, but then there's this," Guimond said as he removed a flash drive from his pocket and plugged it into the laptop computer that he'd brought with him. "The hotel manager gave this to me. Perhaps after you've seen this, you can give me your professional opinion as to whether this case is circumstantial and 'too neat,' as you put it."

When the video came to life, an image of the hallway outside their rooms appeared. At the bottom of the video was a time stamp. Guimond fast-forwarded to 9:02 a.m., when Donati stepped out of his room. The chief inspector was wearing a dark-colored shirt and pants and was carrying a white hotel towel. Sticking out from the edge of the towel was the butt of a handgun.

Donati walked to the end of the hall and knocked on the door of the last room. The hall camera was virtually opposite the room's door, and when the door opened, the victim could be seen standing in the doorway. He didn't seem surprised that Donati was there and waved him inside, after which he closed the door. Ten minutes later, Donati left the room with a crumpled towel in his right hand.

Bruno knew that any jury in the world would convict Donati on what he'd just seen. It had taken the captain only hours to assemble his card hand, but he was holding a royal flush while Donati didn't even have a pair.

CHAPTER 2

ONATI HAD PUT many people behind bars during his career, but he'd never been arrested. Therefore, as he was being led to his cell, this new experience scared him. He felt powerless to prevent his incarceration, apprehensive at being forced to defend himself against charges that were the result of a well-thought-out frame, and depressed at being treated like a criminal.

Because he was a police officer, he was isolated from the general population and placed in the high-security wing of the prison, in a cell by himself. His head was still whirling from what he'd seen at the hotel, and Donati had to tell himself more than once that he wasn't in the middle of a dream and that this was reality. Even though he hadn't yet been questioned, beyond what Guimond had asked him in the victim's room, he'd been an officer long enough to know that a shit storm was headed his way. Therefore, he decided to use his one allowed call to phone his father—the only person he believed could marshal the legal resources to help him. To his credit, the elder Donati kept a cool head and didn't ask a lot of questions. Instead, he said that he'd arrange for an attorney as quickly as possible.

Donati had recognized Abate the instant he'd seen him and immediately believed he'd been set up. He hadn't told Bruno because he had wanted his friend to be able to honestly say that he didn't know the name or occupation of the deceased. The less he knew, the less likely it was that he'd be named an accessory. At least that was Donati's thought process at the time.

Two hours after he phoned his father, he was handcuffed and shackled and taken to a room not far from where he'd been fingerprinted. The room was ten feet on a side, and a black rectangular metal table sat in the center. On either side of it were two matching metal chairs that, like the table, were bolted to a gray concrete floor. Sitting in one of the chairs and waiting for him was a slender man in his late sixties. He was five feet, eight inches in height, had white hair, and wore thin-framed black glasses. His face was oblong, narrowing slightly from his forehead down to his chin. He had a narrow mouth and a long nose, which gave his face the appearance of being longer than it was.

Francois Jubert introduced himself as Donati's attorney. He apologized for having taken so long to see him, but he had decided to first speak with the superintendent of the police force, who was a friend and who had shared the evidence the Paris police had gathered. Donati surmised that what Jubert had been told was bad because the look on his face was as solemn as if he'd just come from a funeral. That conclusion was confirmed when he told Donati about the video, the stolen narcotics in the trunk of his vehicle, and the other evidence the police had assembled in a remarkably short time.

"I've been set up."

"I believe you. But if I'm going to prove that to a jury, I'll need to discredit the substantial amount of evidence the police have against you. Therefore, let's begin with you telling me everything you did from the time you arrived in Paris till the second you were arrested."

And Donati did, also weaving in how he had come to stay at the Ritz Paris, his discovery of the offshore bank account statement, the money wired to the Ritz, and his previous arrest of Abate.

When Donati was finished, Jubert put down his fountain pen on the yellow legal pad on which he'd been writing and looked at Donati with the same solemn look as before. "First of all, let me again affirm that I believe you. I've known your father for decades, and he's spoken of you often. I don't doubt your honesty and integrity or the fact that you've been set up. That said, why would someone spend millions to put you in prison?"

"I don't know."

"I have a very good investigator, Lisette Donais. Let me see what she can uncover. In the meantime, I'll try to get the state's attorney to agree to bail, given your excellent record with the Italian state police. I realize that it's difficult to know that you're an innocent man and that the weight of evidence is against you. But I also believe that the truth will come out and that you'll eventually be exonerated."

The expression on Donati's face didn't change. He believed this to be a platitude, one that he'd heard attorneys give their clients a hundred times before. "I would like your investigator to work closely with Chief Inspector Mauro Bruno," he said. "As you know, he's staying at the Ritz and was, although to a lesser degree, also set up. Please have her call him as soon as possible and arrange for them to meet."

"The police don't have anything yet on Bruno," Jubert said, "or he'd be occupying the cell next to you. However, in my opinion, having him involved, when he is also under suspicion, may not be a wise move."

"I understand the risks. But Mauro Bruno is the best investigator I've ever met. If anyone can get to the truth, he can. I want them to collaborate." He then gave Jubert Bruno's cell phone number, which he'd long ago memorized.

After Guimond departed, Bruno decided to take a walk and think about what had occurred since he arrived in Paris. The day had turned unexpectedly cool, and there was a slight bite in the air as he exited the hotel, turned right, and started toward the Rue de Rivoli. As he did, an athletic-looking man in his late twenties wearing a dark blue sports jacket and tan slacks and carrying a black soft-sided bag over his right shoulder began to follow him. At the same time a black Mercedes Maybach with deeply tinted side and rear windows, which had been parked across the street when Bruno exited the hotel, did a U-turn and also began following him. The chief inspector had followed enough people during his police career to be able to spot a tail, and he took note of both. The Maybach was of particular interest because it might have been the same vehicle that was parked across the street from the hotel when Donati was escorted to a waiting police car.

Bruno picked up his pace and, instead of going to the Rue de Rivoli, made two right turns and entered the Rue Cambon, a one-way street behind the Ritz, walking on the sidewalk facing traffic. If the Maybach was following him, it would have to go through a significant amount of Paris traffic to go around the block and enter the street he was on. The verdict was already in on the athletic-looking man, who was still behind him. Bruno was two-thirds of the way down the block when he noticed the Maybach turning onto the long street. As it approached, he took his cell phone from his pocket and, just before the vehicle was abreast of him, suddenly stepped in front of it, forcing the driver to slam on his brakes. Bruno took a photo of both the license plate and the driver, through the clear front windshield, before returning to the sidewalk. He then walked across the street and took a picture of the athletic-looking man, after which the subject of his photographic zeal sprinted away. Hailing a taxi, Bruno asked the driver to take him to the city prison, wherever that might be.

Twenty minutes later, he was dropped off at La Santé Prison. After finding the visitor entrance and standing in line for twenty minutes to register his request to see Donati, he was told to take a seat in the adjoining waiting room and remain there until he was called. Thirty minutes later, he was escorted by an officer to a large room. The fifty- by thirty-foot room was partitioned down the middle by an inch-thick plexiglass wall. Affixed to either side of it were steel counters three feet from the floor. Ten numbered desk phones, which looked to be from the 1960s, were evenly spaced atop the counter on each side. In front of each phone was a black plastic chair that was bolted to the floor. Bruno was directed to phone number three—the third chair from the left. Looking through the plexiglass, he soon saw a handcuffed and shackled Donati being brought into the room. One of the guards sat him in the chair on the other side of the barrier, removed his cuffs, and affixed another set of cuffs that were attached to a central restraining ring, which gave him enough slack to pick up the phone's handset.

Bruno looked closely at his friend. The normally confident—and what some might consider arrogant—bon vivant was gone.

"I see prison agrees with you," Bruno said, trying to make light of the situation and evoking a weak smile from Donati in return.

"I think it's safe to assume we're on video and being recorded," Donati replied, "so I'll make this short. Francois Jubert is my attorney. If you have any questions for me, please go through him as I'm told the police don't record attorney–client conversations."

Bruno said he understood.

"Mauro," Donati said, in a voice that revealed his worry and concern, "Jubert told me about the purported evidence that the prosecution will try to use to convict me of this murder. After this trial, they will extradite me to Italy to face charges of drug dealing and the murder of my fellow officers. I want to tell you that none of this is true and that someone has spent a substantial amount of time and money to frame me."

"Those last two statements were unnecessary, Elia. I know you're innocent, and we're going to prove it."

"To that end, my attorney is engaging an investigator by the name of Lisette Donais, who will be contacting you. Work with her at your discretion—because in the end, I believe you're the only one who has the skill to find out who's behind this seemingly perfect frame and get the evidence required for my acquittal."

"No frame is ever perfect because its basic premise, that an innocent person is guilty, is false. Peel away the narrative and get to the substance of the matter, and you find out not only who's behind it but also the reason for their endeavor. In fact, I'm happy to say, as Sir Arthur Conan Doyle's alter ego Sherlock Holmes said, that the game is afoot."

After flagging a taxi and asking to be taken to the Ritz, Bruno decided to begin his investigation by focusing on the video that Guimond had shown him. But as the taxi approached the Place Vendôme, he told the driver to pull over and drop him off on the Rue de Rivoli, which was a block away. There he bought several burner phones in the event the police decided to either track him or listen in on his calls with Donati's attorney. He then walked back to the hotel. On his way, he noticed that the Maybach was once again following him, which he viewed as a good sign and necessary if he was to get to the substance of why Donati was being framed and who was behind it.

Upon returning to the hotel, he called the manager. Possibly the most damning evidence against Donati was the surveillance video. There was no doubt in Bruno's mind that it was fake and had somehow been altered. The first step in understanding how that had occurred was to look at the hotel surveillance system and view what Guimond had allegedly downloaded to the flash drive. While he was there, he would see if the hotel's security technician could explain how the video could be altered without anyone knowing about it. Hopefully, the technician could do this in baby language because Bruno considered his computer knowledge to be basic and on par with those seven years of age and below.

As it turned out, the manager of the Ritz was extraordinarily accommodating, especially considering that Bruno had no official police or legal standing in France. The room he was taken to, which housed the hotel's video surveillance system, was to the right of the registration desk, its door protected by a cipher lock. The area was much larger than Bruno had expected. Before him were forty LCD monitors, covering both the interior and the exterior of the hotel. On the opposite wall was a virtual storage device that recorded the data from the entire security camera network. Bruno asked one of the two technicians in the room to look at the 9:00 a.m. video from the hallway outside his and Donati's rooms, and the tech quickly retrieved the video stream. What Bruno saw matched the video Guimond had shown him. Bruno had expected as much but wanted to be thorough and verify that what had been presented to him was accurate. Given his belief that Donati was framed, the only conclusion he could draw was that someone had hacked into the Ritz security camera network and altered the data. There was no other explanation. The problem with that theory was proving it to the satisfaction of the police and possibly a jury. That was a universe beyond his skill level, but not beyond the skill set of the person he would call as soon as he returned to his room.

If Bruno thought that his day couldn't get any worse, he was wrong. When he returned to his room, he found the red message light on his phone flashing. The message was from Dante Acardi, deputy commissioner of the Italian state police, informing him that he was suspended from the force because he was considered a person of interest in a murder investigation. Donati was also suspended, the message informed him, pending the outcome of the trial. Bruno was to immediately hand over his badge and creds to Capitaine Francois Guimond, who would place them in safekeeping.

Five minutes later, there was a knock on the door. When Bruno opened it, he saw Guimond and the athletic man who'd been following him. Without a word Guimond held out his hand, and Bruno, knowing what the gesture meant, took his badge and creds from his pocket and handed them to the captain. There was no joy on Guimond's face as he accepted the items or when he told Bruno that the man accompanying him, whose name was Lieutenant Thibault Garceau, would stay with Bruno the entire time he remained in Paris. No one knew how long that was going to be since Bruno had been told not to leave the city without Guimond's permission.

Thankfully, Bruno had six more days left on his prepaid stay—more if he used the expense money. He briefly thought about moving to a cheaper hotel, which meant any other hotel in the city, but rejected that idea because he didn't believe the police would allow the Ritz to give him whatever credit balance was in the account until they could confirm the source of the funds sent to the hotel.

"I believe you know Lieutenant Garceau," Guimond said, "since you apparently took his photo on the Rue Cambon. He'll be staying in Chief Inspector Donati's room while you're at the hotel. Please make sure the door between your rooms stays open at all times, and don't go anywhere without speaking to him first—even within the hotel."

After Bruno acknowledged what he'd been told, Guimond left. Thirty seconds later, there was a knock on the connecting door to Donati's room, and Bruno unlocked his side, allowing Garceau unobstructed access to both rooms. The problem he now faced was how to make the phone call to his technology geek without Garceau becoming part of the conversation. As it turned out, that was a problem Bruno would not have to solve.

It was one thirty in the morning, half an hour before closing time for the Hemingway Bar at the Ritz Hotel, when the driver of the Maybach, who looked as if he could be on the offensive line of any NFL team, stood from his chair and left the bar. Passing the shopping arcade, he veered left and ascended the plush-carpeted stairway to the first-floor hallway, where he found the room in which Donati had stayed. Knocking on the door several times in rapid succession, he waited for the occupant, who he knew to be Lieutenant Thibault Garceau, thanks to an informant at the police department, to answer. The detective took almost a minute to get to the door and open it, a gun in his hand. But whether because he was startled by the size of the person standing before him or because he was still half asleep, pointing the gun was the only action he took. An instant after the door opened, the Maybach driver grabbed the gun from Garceau's hand and pushed him inside, closing the door behind them. Five minutes later, he left the room and proceeded to the front entrance of the hotel.

The driver of the Maybach returned to the vehicle and drove away from the hotel without saying a word to his employer, which implied that his task had been successful and nothing more needed to be said. The passenger in the back seat was not irritated that the driver had spent the last hour in the hotel. During that time, he'd reclined the first-class airline-style seat and extended his footrest to make himself comfortable while he smoked his cigar. The specially engineered and costly ventilation system he had installed ensured that the air within the vehicle was nearly smoke-free without opening the windows.

The Maybach entered the fifth arrondissement, passed into the Latin Quarter, and eight minutes and 2.9 miles later, drove onto the grounds of the École Normale Supérieure, or ENS, as most Parisians called the country's most prestigious institution of higher learning. It was a Saturday, and only a few of the school's 2,400 students—those who had no social life or wished to focus on their studies—were still on the central Paris campus. The driver stopped the vehicle and opened the rear door for his employer. The six-foot-six man who stepped out was lanky and had disproportionately long legs for his torso. Cesare Rizzo was the spitting image of his late father, Duke Rodolfo Rizzo, albeit forty years younger. He also had the family traits of close-set blue eyes, a fleshy nose, and a voice that sounded like Sam Elliott's. His hair was brown, and he wore it fashionably long in a flow-and-comb style.

Earlier this week, Rizzo had had his bodyguard and driver, Amo Voclain, who was six feet, seven inches tall in his bare feet, stay in the two hotel rooms that Bruno and Donati would soon occupy and install pinpoint wireless cameras in each. Today he had watched on his iPad as Guimond took possession of Bruno's creds and badge, an inevitability for a law enforcement officer who was even tangentially associated with someone accused of a capital crime. However, what he hadn't expected was that the young officer who'd been following Bruno and who now stood beside Guimond would move into Donati's room. Obviously, the police were suspicious of Bruno and thought he might be involved in Abate's killing. This happenstance not only fit precisely with Rizzo's plan but also significantly added to its believability.

Last year Rizzo had been awarded a PhD in computer science from the ENS, just one year after he earned a master's in economics from the same institution. These were the two areas of study that he felt were necessary to successfully invest the family's money, as well as continue its tradition of extortion, thievery, and bribery. His skills in computer science had already paid off when he discovered that he had a natural talent for hacking into computer systems that didn't have the necessary sophistication to protect their data, thereby creating an entirely new revenue vertical for the family, which presently included only himself. However, he intended for that to change. Soon he'd marry and have a family, and his heir would one day succeed him as patriarch and continue to enhance the family's wealth and influence.

He and Voclain walked toward the computer science center, matching each other stride for stride because of their nearly equal height and long legs. However, there the resemblance stopped. Voclain was bald, button-nosed, and brown-eyed, and his clean-shaven face was expressionless. Thick-chested, he had a neck like a tree trunk. The cowboy boots he was addicted to wearing added another inch to his height, giving him a two-inch height advantage over his boss. Duke Rodolfo Rizzo had assigned Voclain to protect his son eighteen years ago in Milan, but seven years ago, the venue had changed to Paris.

The computer science center was housed in the building directly in front of them. Rizzo, who was also a part-time associate professor, had an access card to the building. Upon entering a lab on the ground floor, he turned on a computer. After it came online, he removed a flash drive from his pocket and inserted it. Loading the program he'd designed, he was able to again hack into the computer system of the Ritz Hotel and access the central data storage for its camera systems. For the next five hours, he worked on erasing Voclain's presence in the hotel. Once he was through, he ensured that the backup system also was altered and that the computer logs did not denote his intrusion into the system. Satisfied, he waited for the next part of his plan to unfold.

Bruno awoke at 5:30 a.m. regardless of the day of the week. His body clock was attuned to getting him up at this hour, and he had long ago dispensed with an alarm. He showered, shaved, and got dressed in his customary dark blue suit, white shirt, and light blue tie. Afterward, as he was fixing himself a cup of espresso, he looked at his watch and saw that it was now 6:00 a.m. He decided to see if Garceau wanted to join him. Walking through the connecting doorway to the other room, he immediately saw the lieutenant lying dead on the floor, a gun and a silencer beside him. There was no need to wonder whose gun it was. Bruno knew it was the Beretta 92FS that Donati had given him as a present—the same type of weapon that had been used to kill Abate. He could already guess that his fingerprints were on the weapon and the bullets in the magazine, which meant that as soon as Guimond found out about the murder, Bruno would be occupying the cell beside Donati, if he wasn't killed before then for allegedly killing a police officer. Quickly putting his computer and other personal belongings into a carry-on bag, Bruno left the hotel through the rear exit without checking out.

CHAPTER 3

I T WAS SEVEN o'clock on a Sunday morning, and Lisette Donais was exhausted after following the black Maybach from the Ritz Hotel to the ENS and waiting five hours for the two occupants of the vehicle to return to the vehicle. As they approached the Maybach, she ran back to her black Renault Clio and started the engine. The lithe, D-cupped five-foot-four blonde, who was wearing tight-fitting jeans, a white knit top that some women would feel was a size too small but most men would applaud, and black Steve Madden Ecentrcq sneakers, then pulled away from the curb and followed the Maybach. Moments later, her cell phone rang. There was no caller ID, but that wasn't unusual in her business—many of her informers didn't want their number displayed. Her supermini didn't have Bluetooth, so she put her phone on speaker and placed it in her lap.

The caller introduced himself as Mauro Bruno, whose call Francois Jubert had told her to expect. Bruno said that he was seated at a small bistro across from La Madeleine and needed to see her as soon as possible. As he spoke, the Maybach was gaining speed and heading toward the sixth arrondissement, the most expensive real estate in the city. It was an area where a Maybach wouldn't look out of place, but her Clio would. Donais's division of attention between Bruno and the Maybach wasn't working. She decided to put him on the back burner by saying that she'd meet him at La Madeleine but couldn't promise when because she was following someone. She then ended the call without waiting for a response.

The Maybach entered Saint Germain-des-Prés, proceeded up a street that led to the summit of a hill, and pulled up to a large ornamental wrought iron gate. When the gate retracted, Donais could see a freestone mansion that looked as if it had been built in the eighteenth century. There were numerous windows on each of the four floors, most with private balconies. In front of the mansion was a brick driveway that looped around a huge fountain, where four dolphins spewed a line of water into the center. Three large, brawny men in business suits rushed to the Maybach as soon as it came to a stop, and one opened the back door. As this was happening, one of the men saw her parked across from the entrance and raced out of the compound, causing Donais to make a quick U-turn and speed away just before he could grab her vehicle.

After seeing one of his guards chase after the Renault, Rizzo entered his mansion and, accompanied by Voclain, went straight to the control room, where his security staff monitored the property's surveillance cameras. Although the driver got away before someone could question her, the security cameras got the license plate number of the vehicle along with her photo.

An hour later, Voclain entered Rizzo's living room–style office with two printouts, thanks to a bribe. The first showed that the car was registered to Lisette Donais and gave her address. The second was a copy of her investigator's license along with a short narrative indicating that she was primarily employed by the law firm representing Elia Donati.

"Find Lisette Donais and squeeze from her everything she knows. She's spying on me for a reason—find out why. Once you've extracted all she knows, take her outside the city, kill her, and bury the body where it'll never be found," Rizzo said. "But don't use any of my vehicles. Steal one. If a surveillance camera photographs it, or someone sees it near Donais's residence, then it can't be traced back here. And while you're at it, kill the attorney she's working for in case she told him anything."

Voclain said that he understood and left.

Once his bodyguard was gone, Rizzo hooked up a voice changer to his phone and dialed Guimond's cell, a number he'd obtained from the same government contact who had given him the information on Donais. He told Guimond that Garceau had been murdered by Bruno and that the chief inspector was in the process of fleeing the country. He also said that Bruno had hidden something under the artificial begonias on his balcony, which would show that he and Donati had worked together in their illicit enterprise. Rizzo then hung up, took a cigar from his pocket and lit it, and went to sit in his garden while the events he'd orchestrated unfolded.

Jubert had not given Bruno a physical description of Donais. Therefore, he was surprised when someone who could have been Jennifer Aniston's doppelganger, her blonde hair barely touching her shoulders, approached and introduced herself. Bruno noticed that she wore no jewelry, which he found unusual for someone this attractive. With her stunning looks and the way her tight jeans and top flattered her body, he thought she could probably get any information she wanted from a man by merely sitting close to him, whereas he'd have to resort to waterboarding or extraordinary rendition to get the same data.

Donais ordered an espresso, and Bruno held up two fingers to the newly energetic waiter who had run to their table.

"Thank you for meeting me," Bruno said, starting the conversation. "To begin with, you should know that I'll soon be wanted for the murder of Lieutenant Thibault Garceau."

Donais's eyes widened slightly, and her look hardened at this revelation.

"I didn't do it. I've apparently been set up by the same person who framed Chief Inspector Donati."

"How do you know you'll be framed?"

"Because Lieutenant Garceau was occupying the room next to mine at the Ritz, and my gun was next to his body even though I didn't bring it with me to Paris."

"And why was he staying at such an expensive hotel?"

"Capitaine Guimond had him keeping an eye on me. The room was Donati's and was already paid for."

"So both your gun and that of Monsieur Donati somehow ended up in Paris without your knowledge, and both were used in a homicide at the same hotel." Donais's voice indicated that the jury was still out on whether she believed him. "When's the last time you saw your weapon?"

"Literally hours before I arrived in Paris. I've been racking my brain trying to think of how my gun could have gotten here so quickly. The only possibility I have come up with is that at some point someone broke into my residence and switched my gun with another. Therefore, the gun they took would have my prints on it. They probably did the same for

Elia, although they would have had to photograph the handle of his Beretta in advance in order to accurately duplicate the initials on it."

"Quite a theory. What would someone gain by framing you for murder, rather than putting a bullet in your brain?" Donais asked, still sounding as if she didn't fully buy into what she was being told.

"Revenge."

"Then you know who's behind this."

"I believe I know exactly who's behind this," Bruno responded. "But in order for you to understand why I consider him my only suspect, I have to tell you about something Chief Inspector Donati and I experienced in Milan a little over six months ago."

Donais sat back in her chair and crossed her shapely legs, and this movement instantly brought the waiter back to find out if they wanted anything else. Bruno sent him away.

"Roughly six and a half months ago, a man named Luciano Gismondi killed six people in Milan in a single day. Among the victims was my father, the city's chief prosecutor, whose death was made to look like a car accident."

"I'm sorry for your loss," Donais said, sounding as if she genuinely meant it. "I hope you killed him."

"He's dead."

"The obvious question is, why kill so many people? What did the killer hope to gain?"

"He hoped to protect a centuries-old secret for his employer, Duke Rodolfo Rizzo. Interestingly, the thread connecting these deaths was a pair of eighteenth-century financial ledgers from the Vatican. One was accurate, but the second ledger was cooked, as they say. The person who oversaw this embezzlement scheme was Duke Federigo Rizzo, who lived in the mid-eighteenth century. His accomplice was Cardinal Ettore Casaroli, secretary of state to two pontiffs. Federigo Rizzo essentially used money that he and Casaroli embezzled from the Vatican to start the Bank of Rizzo, which until recently was the largest bank in Italy."

"I read about this. Didn't his descendent commit suicide after a newspaper in Rome published excerpts from a diary he kept?"

"Yes. Each patriarch, as those connected to the Rizzo's called the head of the family, kept an ongoing diary. Duke Rodolfo Rizzo's diary admitted to not only these murders but also a long list of other transgressions. As you probably know, the bank collapsed when the shareholders sold the stock en masse and the stock became worthless. After that, the state moved in to preserve depositors' assets."

"Didn't they sell substantially all of Rizzo's assets?"

"You have an excellent memory. The government sued his estate and sold whatever assets they could find, although they never found his art collection, which was generally acknowledged to be on par with the holdings of many museums. An offshore trust, rumored to be owned by a Saudi prince, bought all the estate's assets, including the mansion and the Gulfstream jet."

"Since Rodolfo Rizzo is dead, who do you believe framed both you and Donati?"

"Duke Rodolfo Rizzo's son—Cesare."

"The newspapers never mentioned another family member. They said Rizzo's wife died some time ago and that he lived by himself."

"His son, from what little we know from speaking to one of Duke Rizzo's guards that we later captured, came to Paris seven years ago. Apparently, he and his father went to extraordinary lengths to keep his name and face out of the public eye."

"And you believe that the son wants revenge for the death of his father, just as you did?"

"I do."

"If he's in France, I'll find him."

"That may prove more difficult than you think. I worked with Interpol to do just that, believing he may have his father's artwork, along with other assets that are unknown to us. He's fallen off the grid—no bank accounts, credit cards, driver's license, lease, or mortgage anywhere in Europe or North America. That notwithstanding, from what's happened to us, I firmly believe he's still in Paris, but obviously not using his legal name."

Donais's cell phone chimed, and the waiter seemed to use this as his excuse to return, standing next to her and patiently waiting for her conversation to end. Bruno didn't know who Donais was speaking with, but he was sure she didn't want the waiter to overhear her conversation. He decided to keep the attentive server busy while she spoke.

"I wonder if you can get us something," Bruno said, summoning the server to his side of the table. "You'll have to write this down," Bruno added. The waiter seemed slightly irritated at being told to get out his order pad, but he removed it and his pen from his apron pocket. "We'll both have a large two-thirds caff triple ristretto affogato, two pumps mango, one pump classic, two percent, mango to the second line, three scoops protein, three scoops berries, two scoops matcha, add banana, double blended, with whip, caramel drizzle, salted caramel topping, vanilla bean Frappuccino." The waiter stared in disbelief at what he'd written and left the table still looking at his pad as Donais ended her call.

"That was Monsieur Jubert. He received a call from Guimond, inquiring if he knew your whereabouts. After Jubert said that he didn't, Guimond told him that you're the subject of a manhunt for the murder of Thibault Garceau, just as you expected. Jubert called me in case you had phoned, since he gave you my number."

"What did you tell him?"

"That I hadn't heard from you."

"Why?"

"Because your story is too crazy and convoluted to be a lie and because I don't believe either you or Donati are stupid enough to leave your weapons with your fingerprints or initials on them at the scene of a murder."

"You also should know that when the police search my room, they'll find bank statements for two offshore accounts hidden under the artificial flowers on the balcony—one statement for Donati and one for myself—each with a million dollars in it."

"Donati told Monsieur Jubert about his offshore bank statement, but he didn't mention yours. It's inevitable that the police will eventually find out about your account, whether through an anonymous tip or from someone sending them a copy of your statement. I'm almost sure Guimond believes that both you and Donati are drug dealers who were jointly involved in Abate's death. He'll also believe that you were afraid of being arrested and therefore decided to kill Garceau and get away while you had the opportunity."

"I know how bad this is. Given the evidence, it's going to be hard to prove our innocence."

"After Monsieur Jubert gave me this assignment, I decided to stake out your hotel and follow you if you left," Donais said, without preamble.

"You didn't trust me. I don't blame you."

"I didn't trust you," Donais admitted. "Although I didn't see you leave the hotel after you returned from La Santé Prison, I did notice a black Mercedes Maybach parked across the Place Vendôme from your hotel."

"I saw that Maybach parked there twice, once when Donati was being arrested. I took a photo of it," Bruno said, pulling his cell phone from his pocket and showing it to Donais.

Donais nodded slightly when she saw the photo of the driver. She confirmed that he was one of the people she had seen at the ENS and that the license plate on the photographed Maybach matched the one she had followed to the campus of the École Normale Supérieure.

"Can you describe Cesare's father?" Donais asked.

Bruno gave her a description of the duke and watched as her expression turned pensive.

"The person I saw get out of the back of the Maybach early this morning matched that description too."

"Cesare?"

"That would be my guess. I followed him to an enormous residence in the Saint Germain-des-Prés area of Paris—the most exclusive area of the city."

"Sounds like he has the same expensive taste as his father. Now we know where he's living."

"Possibly. When I left the area, I pulled over and was able to access the city's property tax database records for that residence from my cell phone. It's owned by a Saudi offshore trust. That's a far cry from the scion of an Italian banker."

"Cesare Rizzo probably has enough money to obfuscate anything. It's too much of a coincidence that he bears so much resemblance to Rodolfo Rizzo and resides in Paris."

Donais suddenly looked at Bruno's phone in the same way she might have looked at a venomous snake. Quickly grabbing the iPhone, she threw it on the ground and smashed it using her chair leg.

"We have to leave now," Donais said, throwing a twenty-euro note on the table and handing Bruno his travel bag. "I should have thought about your phone earlier."

Bruno shook his head and unconsciously touched one of the burner phones in his pocket. The look of disgust on his face indicated that he knew he'd screwed up in not leaving his phone at the hotel—when tracking a suspected murderer, the first thing law enforcement would do is find what cell tower his phone was pinging.

Bruno didn't have a chance to think about his situation for long because when he looked up, the fleet-footed Donais was already twenty yards away and almost to her vehicle. He quickly grabbed his carry-on bag and followed her. By the time he got into the vehicle, she had her seat belt on and was putting the Renault in gear. As they cut down a side street and merged onto the Champs-Elysées, they saw a dozen police cars racing in the opposite direction, toward the area they'd just left.

Guimond had gotten everything he could from the waiter about the identity of the woman with Bruno—which was to say nothing since the server hadn't looked at her face that closely, focusing instead on other areas of her anatomy. Nevertheless, the captain had a good idea who she might be. He'd go to her residence later and see if she was there and ask her about the fugitive inspector.

Bruno's smashed cell phone meant that Guimond could no longer track the Italian inspector. Nevertheless, he'd give the phone to his techies and see what they could recover from its remains. Forensics would arrive shortly, although the waiter said that the espresso cups that Bruno and the mystery woman had drunk from had already been taken to the kitchen and placed in the washer. The two large coffee drinks on the table, which looked to be untouched, were another matter. He motioned to the waiter.

"What are these?"

"These were ordered by the man you said you were looking for."

"He ordered these, then neither he nor the woman drank them?"

"They left before I brought these to the table."

Curious, Guimond took a sip, then a much larger one. Eventually, he drained the glass. "This is quite extraordinary," he told the waiter. "Do you have the recipe?"

The waiter gave it to him, after which Guimond asked if he could take the second drink in a go-cup.

Donais drove down a narrow street lined with apartment buildings that tended to be in the lower end of the residential retail market. Most of the units in the area had been built just after World War II during a surge to construct affordable housing and therefore had none of the spacious elegance associated with the wealthier and more fashionable residences of the city. She pulled in front of a steel accordion gate beside one of these buildings, then got out of her car and used one of the keys on her keyring to unlock it. She slid the gate aside, climbed back into the car, and drove into a small parking garage that appeared to be beneath several of the second-floor residences, parking her supermini in the space with the number 1F painted in the center. After relocking the gate, she and Bruno walked to the front door of the building.

"This is my grandmother's apartment," Donais said, "and I look in on her from time to time. She left last week to visit her sister in Lyon and won't be back for another two."

Bruno didn't verbally respond but nodded his understanding. He followed her to the building entrance, where she used the garage key to open the door. The hallway in front of them was well lit, and Bruno saw that it ended at an elevator. Apartment 1F was the first residence on the left. Donais selected another key from her keyring and opened the door.

The residence was small—one bedroom, one bathroom, a kitchen, and a living room, a total of 750 square feet. The living room contained a two-cushion sofa, in front of which was a rectangular coffee table, and two thickly padded armchairs to the side, each with a blue crocheted cover. The furniture was old and heavy, having long ago gone out of style. Despite the furniture's age, each piece appeared to be well cared for, with not a scratch visible.

"We can stay here until we sort things out," Donais said.

"I take it you can't go home because Guimond knows you're helping me."

"When the waiter gives him my description, Luc will know it was me."

"Luc?"

"We used to be an item."

Bruno stopped his questioning, and Donais walked to the couch and sat down, folding her legs under herself. Bruno took a seat in the armchair closest to her.

"Eventually, they'll find us," Donais said. "Paris has a very sophisticated camera system that utilizes facial recognition software. The longer we're outside the apartment, the higher the chance of discovery. The police will also start visiting my relatives and known associates. I'd estimate we have at most a day or two until they come here."

"Then we have twenty-four to forty-eight hours to get the proof necessary to clear Donati and me."

"This sounds like the premise for a *Mission Impossible* movie. Any ideas where to start?"

"One," Bruno said, taking out one of his burner phones and calling Montanari.

CHAPTER 4

NDRO MONTANARI WAS an electrical engineering and computer savant who made his living hacking into computer systems and getting around electronically controlled barriers to entry. These skills had earned him a fortune until the day Mauro Bruno arrested him. Sentenced to prison, he had been three years away from parole when he was summoned late one night to take a phone call from the person who'd sent him to jail. Bruno's reason for calling was to ask him how to bypass an RFID system—the same crime that had gotten him incarcerated. Nevertheless, Montanari had provided the technical information, enabling Bruno to expose Duke Rodolfo Rizzo and his family tree for the centuries of crimes they'd committed. In return, Bruno not only had Montanari's sentence commuted but also got him his first client for his fledging security consulting business: the Vatican.

Montanari answered his cell, even though the call was from an unfamiliar number. When he asked who was calling, he was surprised to find out that it was Bruno, whose cell number was stored in his phone. Obviously, the chief inspector was using another phone, a detail that immediately piqued his curiosity.

Bruno started by explaining that he and Donati were in Paris and went on to summarize what had happened and the evidence that the police had in their possession. "And if they altered security footage to frame Donati," Bruno continued, "I'm certain that they have done the same to me. I don't believe I'm wrong in suggesting that the hotel's camera feed from this morning will show that the hallway outside the room of the person that I supposedly killed was empty the entire night, and therefore I was the only person who could have killed him, since no one else was seen entering the victim's room. This is on top of the fact that Donati and I, as I explained, somehow have a million dollars each in offshore bank accounts."

"It's obvious that whoever did this hacked the hotel's data storage system and manipulated the video surveillance data," Montanari said. "That's the bad news. The good is that there are several ways to debunk the video that the police believe seals the case against Chief Inspector Donati. As you know, in my previous profession I hacked into many computer-controlled security systems. Once inside, I suspended the cameras or looped a recording so that everything appeared normal. However, I never bothered to erase or change the video because I knew an expert could show that changes had been made. Changes are virtually impossible to hide from a trained eye."

"Explain that," Bruno said.

"When we talk about security cameras, there are two types of video inconsistencies, physical and electronic. Addressing those that are physical, we know that someone other than Donati entered the Ritz, killed this drug dealer, and left. The murderer, or one of his accomplices, then altered the image stream from the hallway camera outside your room and substituted Donati for the killer. For the moment, let's set aside the technical aspects of how this can be accomplished—just know that it can done. If what you told me about the extensive camera coverage of the hotel is accurate, there should be a recording of the killer entering and leaving the hotel, as well as walking up to the first-floor hallway. The person who did this wouldn't have had time to alter the entire video file. The image substitution and elimination that he did to frame Donati was probably already pushing the edge of his time envelope. I'm also guessing that the security cameras of the businesses and government offices adjacent to the Ritz will have video, even if it's at a distance, of those entering and leaving the hotel."

"The Ministry of Justice is next door," Bruno confirmed.

"Good. These other cameras could provide possible exculpatory evidence because whoever committed these murders is going to be seen on one of these camera systems going into and out of the hotel, but they won't be visible on the Ritz's internal camera system," Montanari said. "In other words, you won't see them inside."

"And the electronic inconsistencies?" Bruno asked.

"Too complicated to go into in detail, but it involves the laws of physics and optics. Those will be impossible for the prosecutor to disprove. Trust me on this, Mauro. The police believe that the video they have will prove Donati's guilt. On the contrary, it'll be evidence of his innocence. It shouldn't take me long to gather this information for you."

"I appreciate the offer, Indro, but I called for your advice, not your involvement. Hacking is illegal and will get you thrown back into jail. You have a life now—don't ruin it."

There was a slight pause in the conversation before Montanari responded.

"I'm not walking away, Mauro. You helped me turn my life around. Now it's time for me to help you and Donati. Here's what I need."

Givon Messai was technically a member of the Saudi royal family, although the amount of royal blood in him could probably be measured in drops, which was why he was working and not jet-setting around the world. Nevertheless, this trace amount ensured that he received a substantial salary, enough to support he and his wife, for merely showing up for work. At five feet three he was nearly four inches below the average height for a Saudi and fifty pounds over the average weight— not exactly the poster boy for the House of Saud or a lady-killer.

One day Messai was having lunch at his usual table at a restaurant near his office when he was approached by a stunning woman who said that she was a French journalist. She spoke excellent Arabic and asked if she could join him, since she hated eating alone. Not about to turn down the opportunity to dine with a beautiful woman, he replied that he also hated eating by himself. Once they had introduced themselves and briefly discussed their professions, Messai ordered a bottle of champagne, and they spent the next two hours eating, drinking, and talking. The quasi royal, who was thinking with the lower section of his anatomy rather than his brain, asked if she would like to continue their discussion over another bottle of champagne at the hotel across the street. To his astonishment, she accepted, and so began their weekly tryst. Four weeks after they began their affair, he heard knocking on the hotel room door. Assuming it was his lover, he opened the door, dressed in nothing but a robe and slippers. However, instead of the stunning woman he was expecting, it was a six-foot-six man with long legs. He offered no salutation or introduction. The man simply told him that his lover wasn't coming and entered the hotel room uninvited. He then put the computer he was carrying on the desk, opened the screen, and brought up a video. Messai stared at the screen in disbelief—it showed him and the journalist having sex in the bedroom. Given the angle, the camera must have been on the nightstand where his lover had always placed her large purse.

"I don't have to tell you," the man said, "that the royal family doesn't like adverse publicity, especially affairs. If this video was made public, you'd lose your job and come under investigation by the religious police, your wife would divorce you, and the king could lop off your head to show his people that no one is above the law."

Messai's knees buckled, and his face turned white as he fell back onto the couch. Pleading with the stranger, he asked what it would take for him to destroy the video.

The man reached into the breast pocket of his jacket and removed a completed passport application, a birth certificate for a child who'd died weeks before, and a headshot photo of himself. The stranger then told him what he wanted. Later that day, the man who would now call himself Gamal Al-Mutairi received his passport, whereupon he invited Messai to dinner as a way of thanking him for what he'd done.

The quasi royal, who never wanted to see the stranger again, accepted the invitation because he was too scared to refuse. Halfway through the dinner, while Messai was in the restroom relieving himself of the half bottle of Cristal champagne he'd consumed, the other man emptied a small packet of ricin into his champagne. Two days later, after suffering from an apparent bad bout of flu, the lowest-ranking member of the House of Saud was dead.

Cesare Rizzo, known now as Gamal Al-Mutairi, stared out the front window of his Saint Germain-des-Prés mansion, occasionally taking a puff from his cigar. He had moved to Paris seven years ago. Obtaining a Saudi passport hadn't been a must, but it did stifle questions as to the origin of his money because everyone assumed that Saudis were inherently wealthy. Almost any other nationality he could have impersonated would have invited unwanted questions. Therefore, he had traveled to Saudi Arabia as himself, enlisted a high-priced prostitute to impersonate a journalist, and paid her double her usual fee to go along with the charade. Picking Messai hadn't been difficult. Rizzo's research had shown that there were three government officials who could unilaterally issue a Saudi passport. All these positions were held by men, and all three had foibles that made them easy extortion targets. Rizzo didn't particularly look like a Saudi, but that didn't matter because he was so wealthy that everyone wanted to believe he was.

Rizzo took a last puff from his cigar, set it on a silver tray on the small table to his right, and poured himself a finger of Hennessy Beauté du Siécle Grand Champagne cognac, his father's favorite. It was only a matter of time until Bruno was captured or killed by a zealous police officer wanting to avenge Garceau's death. Where could he go? With the entire French police force looking for him, he wouldn't last long. Rizzo's game plan was to have Bruno and Donati die in disgrace, amid the same social stigma they'd inflicted on his father. To that end, Rizzo had indirectly provided police with enough information to convict each. The only fly in the ointment that Rizzo could see was Donais, because he had no idea how long she'd been following him or what she knew. That's why she had to be eliminated. In his experience, information spread logarithmically, which was why she had to be killed quickly, before she had time to tell anyone what she knew. Summoning Voclain, Rizzo told the bodyguard what needed to be done and left the details up to him.

The hearing for Donati's bail didn't go as Jubert had planned. Noting that Donati was a distinguished law enforcement officer in Italy with no prior arrests and that he was pleading innocent to murdering Abate, the distinguished French attorney argued that his client was not a flight risk and should be given bail. Those statements took thirty seconds. The district attorney then stood and opposed bail, reporting that the prosecution had a video of Donati entering Abate's room with a gun at approximately the same time the coroner said the victim was killed. In addition, the police in Milan said that they'd found sixty kilos of heroin in the trunk of Donati's car, drugs that previously had been confiscated by police from Abate. The district attorney therefore concluded that Donati was the definition of a flight risk because he could spend the rest of his life in jail for either of these crimes. That argument took one minute. The judge then decided that he'd heard enough. He banged his gavel, denied bail, and called the next case. Immediately afterward, the officer standing behind Donati stepped forward, put handcuffs on the inspector, and led him through a door at the side of the courtroom as Jubert watched.

Jubert stuffed his papers back in his briefcase and took the elevator down to the parking garage. He drove his Citroën C3 to the exit, inserted his keycard into the slot, watched the barrier arm raise in front of him, and drove out of the courthouse lot. At that moment, his car window was hit by a large rock—or at least that was his initial thought until he felt a sharp pain in his chest. Looking down, he saw blood coming from a wound. Barely able to think and feeling himself becoming light-headed, he slumped to the side. Fifteen seconds later, half the time it had taken him to argue for bail, he was dead.

CHAPTER 5

MONTANARI BELIEVED FROM the start that getting the Ritz Paris camera data would be difficult because the hotel, given its elite clientele, would have hired only the most competent software consultants to design and install its firewalls and security protocols. That prediction was correct. Even with his master algorithm, which had penetrated the Italian government's computer system and that of many corporations as easily as a hot knife cut through butter, it took him several hours to hack the Ritz's server, more than twice the time that he had expected. Once inside the system, he downloaded the security camera's data from the time Donati checked into the hotel until Bruno snuck out the back door. He then began his search for physical and electronic inconsistencies, beginning with the episode involving Bruno.

The first inconsistency he found involved a large man, six feet six or taller. Montanari followed him as he walked into the hotel and proceeded to Hemingway's Bar, which was in the rear on the ground floor. The man wasn't in the bar for long, and once he left, a security camera showed that instead of retracing his steps to the hotel exit, he ascended the rear staircase to the first floor. What made this particularly interesting was that the first-floor hallway camera never saw him, even though several minutes later the lobby camera had him descending the front staircase at the other end of the hall. That was at 2:00 a.m. Based on this, Montanari believed that he was looking at Garceau's killer. Now he needed to focus on who had killed Abate and framed Donati.

Finding the inconsistencies relating to Donati's purported murder of Abate wasn't difficult because Montanari again saw the same man enter the hotel not long after Donati had checked in. Just as before, he went to the first floor by way of the back staircase, this time carrying a Hermes shopping bag. The paper bag seemed to be holding something because there was a slight bulge on the side.

Whatever business this man had on the first floor didn't take long because he descended the front staircase to the lobby only ten minutes later. The Hermes bag was still in his right hand, but it was clearly empty when he laid it flat on one of the end tables that he passed. Montanari believed that this second inconsistency showed that the tall man had also killed Abate. Next, he'd search for pixelation vagaries to better document his findings.

Since images were nothing more than a sequential flow of colored dots, Montanari modified the search parameters of his algorithm to look for color changes—in this case, those in a person's face. Since the heart pumps blood throughout the body, and a computer-generated image doesn't have a heartbeat, a computer-modified face will never become flush or change its pixelation. It always remains the same. And this is exactly what the reformed thief saw when Donati supposedly walked down the hall—there wasn't even the slightest change in color from the pumping of blood or the slight physical exertion of walking down the hall. This latest inconsistency meant that Donati's image was superimposed over that of the killer.

The next pixelation test involved looking at shadows. Again, Montanari modified the search parameters of his program to look for inconsistencies in this area. Almost without exception, when an object such as a person is inserted into a video or photo, the shadow of the object or person will be in the wrong place because the geometry of light striking the body and the subsequent creation of shadows are different. In the case of Donati walking down the hall, there was a shadow of his left forearm, hip, and leg. Montanari stopped the video when Donati was directly beneath a hallway light. He then drew on his computer screen, with an erasable marker, a line from Donati's forearm, hip, and leg to his shadow. These three lines should have converged on the overhead light source. The laws of geometry demanded it. However, they didn't. Therefore, since the shadow in the video was geometrically impossible, the image of Donati had to have been inserted. The third pixelation test involved the chief inspector's eyes. The hallway light should have been reflected in the center of his eyes, but this was not the case. Instead, the reflections were on the right side.

Montanari again returned to Bruno. The hotel video showed that no one was in the first-floor hallway at the time Garceau was killed. Therefore, there shouldn't have been any inconsistencies with brightness in the hall. Again adjusting the search parameters of his algorithm, he saw areas of solid black. The problem with this was that solid black does not technically exist, because even deep black has various ranges of brightness and is not uniform. In combination, his findings were solid proof that the data from the camera security system at the Ritz had been altered. Consequently, he had more than enough evidence to clear both Bruno and Donati. The only obstacle to his handing this information to the police was the legal term "fruit of the poisonous tree," which meant that if the source of the evidence was tainted, then anything gained from it was tainted as well. In other words, if the information from the Ritz was illegally obtained, it probably wouldn't be admitted into evidence. Moreover, he'd go to jail for computer hacking. Of course, all bets were off if the police received the information from an anonymous source.

Having killed Jubert, Voclain now needed to question Donais and find out everything she knew about his employer, then kill her and get rid of her body, just as Rizzo had instructed. He had no desire to spend hours in his car staking out her apartment or loitering in the area around her building. His size made him anything but inconspicuous, and when Donais's body was eventually found or she was declared missing, people would remember seeing him and would give his description to the police. Removing his cell phone from his pocket, he called the government official who had earlier sent him the information on Donais and asked him to get Donais's cell phone number as well as her present location. Ten minutes later, he was back in his vehicle and putting the address given to him in the car's navigation system. He now headed away from the glitzier area of Paris. Crossing the Canal Saint-Denis and the Canal de l'Ourcq, he entered the heart of the nineteenth arrondissement, which was largely an immigrant community.

The address given to him was on a narrow street lined with tired apartment buildings. Parking his car fifty yards from the building, he saw Guimond, the same officer who had arrested Donati, walking to the front entrance of the building.

Voclain watched as Guimond pressed the call button above the first mailbox and bent down and said something into the speaker. A minute later, he opened the front door and entered the building.

Bruno saw the confusion and fear in Donais's face when the apartment buzzer rang. He didn't have to ask her what the sound meant—someone was at the front door. Hopefully, whoever was there wanted to see Donais's grandmother, not knowing she was away. But odds were that it was the police. There were undoubtedly making it a priority to search all possible locations looking for them, beginning with family and friends—the same thing Bruno would have done if the situation were reversed.

Bruno pulled back the drapes a sliver and looked out the side window. He saw a police car double-parked near the entry door and Guimond standing near the buzzer.

"It's Guimond," Bruno said.

"The building has a rear exit," Donais replied. "Quickly. We can be a block away before he gets the manager to open this door."

"And then what? There's no place to hide. You go. I'm the one he's after."

This time it was Donais who parted the drapes and looked. "It seems odd that he's alone. If he were really searching for a cop killer, he'd have two or three officers accompanying him. There's something more."

"You said that you and Luc were once an item. Maybe he's here to speak with you and doesn't know I'm here. Let him in, and I'll give my side of the story. At least I'll be alive when they throw me in the cell next to Donati. If another officer sees me, they'll shoot first and then ask my corpse for an explanation as to what happened, if you get my point."

Donais pressed the button to let Guimond into the building. Soon after, there was a knock, and Donais opened the door. Guimond appeared happy to see her, giving her a kiss on both cheeks and complimenting her on how beautiful she looked. It wasn't until she fully opened the door and Bruno came into view that a diametrically opposite expression appeared on his face. Drawing his gun, he ordered Bruno to raise his hands and interlock his fingers behind his head. Bruno complied. Guimond was in the process of removing his cell phone from his pocket when Donais gently touched his arm.

"Put the phone away, Luc. He didn't kill anyone," Donais said, closing the door. Walking toward Bruno, she told him to go sit in the chair and asked Guimond to take a seat on the couch.

Guimond insisted on frisking Bruno before either man sat down.

"It's not what you think, Luc," Donais began.

"What I think is that the person I'm looking at murdered an innocent police officer, because the hotel video shows that there was no one in the hall outside Garceau's room at the time the coroner said he was killed. That means the killer had to be Bruno. What happened, Chief Inspector—did Garceau look under the begonias on the balcony and find the bank statements for the million-dollar accounts? Did he confront you with it? Is that when you decided to kill him?"

Bruno was surprised at Guimond's discovery, although he'd previously told Donais that he believed the statements he'd hidden would eventually be found.

"Chief Inspector Bruno didn't kill anyone. Let me tell you what I saw the night Garceau was killed," Donais said. She proceeded to tell Guimond about the person she had followed and what she suspected.

"Lisette, following someone to the ENS and then to their home can only be considered interesting. And the fact that the person you followed physically resembles Duke Rodolfo Rizzo is also nothing more than interesting. Where's the crime?"

"We're trying to get proof that the video surveillance at the Ritz was altered to frame both Bruno and Donati."

"Don't you think I had the video checked to see if it had been altered? Two of my technicians looked at it, and both concluded that it hadn't been tampered with. They'll testify to that in court."

"No disrespect meant," Bruno said, butting into their conversation, "but are they experienced at detecting the subtleties of video alteration?"

"One graduated at the top of his computer class, and the other has been the head of our information technology department for the past fifteen years."

The quizzical look that Bruno gave Guimond indicated that he didn't believe either man was qualified to determine whether video alteration had occurred.

"In any event, Lisette, it's out of my hands. This man is a fugitive, and I'm taking him down to the station and charging him with the murder of Lieutenant Garceau. In my report, I'll state that the chief inspector came to you for help and that you called me." Guimond looked over at Bruno. "Do you have a problem with that story?"

When Bruno said that he didn't, Guimond asked him to stand and then cuffed him. With Donais following, Guimond led Bruno out the apartment door.

CHAPTER 6

AFTER HE WATCHED Guimond enter the building, Amo Voclain raced to the apartment house to look at the first postal box, which would give him the apartment that Guimond was going to. He saw that it was apartment 1F, but no name was listed. As he was turning to return to his car, the front door opened, and Guimond led a handcuffed Bruno outside, with Donais following the two men. At that point, all four people were staring at each other. Bruno and Donais would later say that what happened next occurred so fast that no one had time to think, and everyone just reacted.

Donais screamed to Guimond, "That's the person I saw coming out of the hotel the night Garceau was killed!"

At the same time, Bruno yelled, "Arrest him!"

Guimond was processing all this as Voclain turned and ran, pulling out his gun as he raced back toward the vehicle he'd stolen earlier. Seeing this, Guimond withdrew his weapon and shot twice at the fleeing man, missing high both times, before Voclain returned fire. This forced Guimond, Bruno, and Donais to dive to the ground to avoid being hit. When they looked up, Voclain had made a U-turn and was speeding away.

"Are you all right?" Guimond asked, helping Donais to her feet and leaving Bruno, still in handcuffs, to fend for himself.

"I'm fine. As I said, that's the person I saw coming out of the Ritz at 2:00 a.m., around the time Garceau was murdered. The question you have to ask is, why did he shoot at us?"

"I can't answer that," Guimond confessed.

"I can," Bruno said. "The killer was following you to try to locate Donais. He wants to kill her because she can place him at the hotel at the time of the murder and also link him to his boss."

"Do you know the name of the person who shot at us?" Guimond asked.

"Not yet," Bruno answered. "I've been trying to avoid arrest. I didn't think I'd be able to clear myself or Donati if I was thrown in jail. That, and I wasn't sure I'd be allowed to surrender since cop killers are normally killed on sight."

The look on Guimond's face said that he thought the same. "I have no reason to trust you, but I do trust Lisette," Guimond said. "However, if I find out that you've betrayed either of us, I'll kill you—in self-defense, of course. Do we understand each other?"

Bruno said that he did, and Guimond removed his cuffs.

"Lisette, you're in charge of him. You have two days to get me evidence that Bruno didn't murder Garceau and Donati didn't kill Abate. I can't give you cover any longer than that, not with the entire city looking for him. If you can't come up with anything substantial and verifiable in forty-eight hours, then I expect you to bring him to me so that he can turn himself in. Agreed?"

Both Donais and Bruno nodded their agreement.

"You'll both need somewhere to stay. I can let you use a safe house that the police keep in the fourth arrondissement on the Île Saint-Louis. Here's the address," Guimond said, writing on a piece of paper and handing it to Donais. "I'll take the residence out of rotation so that no one will bother you while you're there. You'll also need transportation, so take my car. Do you still have a key to my apartment?"

Donais confessed that she did.

"Then you know where I keep my car keys. If you need my help in the next forty-eight hours, I'll do all I can to assist you without compromising myself. Just remember—at the end of that time, you hand him over to me."

Guimond put them in the back of his police vehicle and dropped them off at his residence. Before she got out of the car, Donais leaned in and gave him a kiss on the lips.

"Bon chance," Guimond said.

A moment later, he drove away.

The Île Saint-Louis was a natural island in the Seine River, connected to the rest of Paris by four bridges. The island was quiet and upscale, with seventeenth- and eighteenth-century buildings containing primarily multimillion-dollar apartments rather than businesses. Interspersed with these, bordering narrow streets lined by tall trees that evoked a feeling of wealth and elegance, were upscale cafés and restaurants. Bruno guessed that the reason this safe house was so secure was that no one expected the police to have a $4 million residence overlooking the Seine.

Looking in the large kitchen, Bruno opened the refrigerator and the freezer and saw that both were well stocked, and the cupboards contained a variety of canned foods.

"I've given this some thought," Bruno said, walking through the kitchen and taking a seat in one of the club chairs in the great room, which overlooked the river. Donais sat in a matching chair beside him. "You said that the Maybach went from the Ritz to the ENS campus. That's where you saw the person who I believe to be Cesare Rizzo, along with the man who shot at us today."

Donais nodded her agreement.

"What were they doing there at two in the morning? It wasn't to attend class. And I don't believe they broke into the building given the time they spent inside and the fact that they didn't trip an alarm, so how were they able to gain access?"

"Two possibilities stand out," Donais replied. "Either they met someone, or they were there to use university equipment capable of hacking into the Ritz camera system and altering the data stored in the hard drive."

"That might answer a lot of questions," Bruno said.

Over the next hour, they dissected the events of the past two days. Their discussion was interrupted, however, when one of Bruno's burner phones rang. Since he'd given that number to only one person, he answered knowing that it would be Guimond. They spoke for several minutes, with Bruno taking notes during their conversation. When the call ended, Bruno turned to Donais, who was still in the club chair beside him, and repeated what Guimond had told him.

"Guimond says that the name of the person who shot at us is Amo Voclain. A street surveillance camera photographed him in a stolen vehicle a block from your grandmother's apartment. He arrived in France seven years ago from Saudi Arabia, but he has an Italian passport. He's currently employed as a driver for a man named Gamal Al-Mutairi, at least according to information stored in the government's database. The police have issued a warrant for his arrest. Gamal Al-Mutairi arrived in Paris at the same time as Voclain. Interestingly, he received a PhD from the ENS and is finishing his master's in economics."

"What's his PhD in?"

"Computer science," Bruno answered with a smile.

"Looks like we may have our hacker. And given his resemblance to Duke Rodolfo Rizzo, it seems likely that Gamal Al-Mutairi is an alias for Cesare Rizzo. That would certainly explain his ax to grind against you and Donati. I find it difficult to believe that his Saudi passport is real."

"Guimond checked. The Saudi government's computer system verified that it's authentic."

"I'm not buying it," Donais said. "There is a reason Voclain was at the hotel the night Garceau was killed and also shot at us. It only makes sense if Rizzo is Gamal Al-Mutairi. We have our killer and the person he works for."

"The problem is, we have no proof. Guimond can arrest Voclain for the attempted murder at your grandmother's apartment and for driving a stolen vehicle, but not for murdering Abate or Garceau. In any scenario, Rizzo will be in the clear unless Voclain gives him up, which I believe is unlikely given their apparent relationship." With a look of frustration on his face, Bruno stood. "Is there any wine in this apartment?" he asked.

"*Certainement,*" Donais replied. "This is France. You might not find bottled water, but wine, always."

CHAPTER 7

"WE'VE ACCOMPLISHED WHAT we wanted," Rizzo said to Voclain after the latter explained what had happened at the apartment building. "Bruno and Donati are still in an untenable position, and based on the surveillance videos, they'll be convicted. Seeing them spend the rest of their lives in jail won't balance the scales for what they did to my father, but it will go a long way toward it."

"Once Bruno is arrested, I can have him and Donati killed while they're in jail."

"As tempting as that is, let them rot in prison for the remainder of the lives. That will give me a great deal of satisfaction."

"We do have a problem that needs to be addressed. The police have my description and will be searching for me. Eventually, they'll discover my identity and that I work for you."

"That's an easy problem to solve. You'll have to die."

Voclain gave him a worried look.

"Figuratively, of course," Rizzo continued.

Relief was apparent on Voclain's face, which went from taut to relaxed.

"Do you still have your friend at the Unione Corse?" Rizzo asked, referring to the Corsican mafia organization through which Voclain brokered weapons smuggling and other illegal activities on behalf of Rizzo.

Voclain said that he did.

"Then tell them that we need a body matching your physical attributes to be consumed in the fiery crash of a stolen car. But make clear that some remnants of your passport and driver's license must survive. I want them to identify you as the immolated driver of the vehicle."

"When do you need this to happen?"

"By morning. We need the police to stop searching for you as soon as possible. Otherwise, they'll start taking a close look at me."

"And once I'm dead?"

"We leave France. I moved here to be close to my father and watch over the family assets, most of which were transported out of Italy over a period of time to protect them. Now that he's gone, there's no reason to remain in Paris. I need a more robust business environment for our legitimate and nonlegitimate enterprises. That means it's time to move to our new home."

Montanari hacked into the Paris police department's computer system in a fraction of the time it had taken to bypass the Ritz's firewall. Finding Guimond's private email, he sent his analysis of the Ritz video along with relevant snippets that documented his findings. He also gave the captain the names of three imagery experts, whose findings were regarded by their peers as the word of God. Montanari knew that anyone with expertise in video or imagery analysis would come to the same conclusions he'd drawn. And once they did, Donati and Bruno would no longer be suspects. The email he sent was untraceable, thereby ensuring his privacy.

He expected pushback from the local techs who had first looked at the video, the ones who had summarily declared Bruno and Donati guilty because they hadn't spotted the numerous discrepancies in the altered video stream. It was unlikely that they'd agree with his conclusions, which would be like saying, "Look how stupid we were—but you should still trust us with people's lives in the future." This was why Montanari gave Guimond the other imagery experts' names.

After he finished, Montanari grabbed a Red Bull and went back to the project he'd been working on before Bruno called.

Guimond knew that everyone lied—both the innocent and the guilty. Whether they did it out of a desire to seem perfect and free of human frailties or to cover their guilt with a protestation of innocence, everyone had their own agenda. Therefore, he looked at the anonymous email with a great deal of skepticism. The sender had provided an analysis, supported by attachments, that explained in detail how the Ritz's camera data had been altered and, subsequently, why Bruno and Donati were innocent. Although the explanation made sense, the simple fact was that Guimond didn't have the expertise to know if what he was being shown was tech smoke and mirrors or the truth. Since the two techs who'd already evaluated the video stream had made their position clear, Guimond believed that he needed an impartial analysis. The last thing he wanted to do was go into court and have a defense attorney shred his techs during depositions and trial. He therefore needed to get what had been sent to him into the hands of someone with an unblemished reputation in analyzing imagery and video data. He didn't have the vaguest idea of who that might be, but the sender apparently had anticipated his dilemma and did know some people.

Going through the three names provided, Guimond researched each and discovered that all were well-documented experts with international reputations for analyzing video data streams. He called the first person on the list, and after a brief conversation, the woman accepted his invitation to come to the police station and look at the video and the analysis that accompanied it.

An hour later, Claudine Noel, five feet, six inches tall with chestnut hair that flowed down to her shoulders, blue eyes, and an athletic physique, walked into his office. She was attractive, appeared to be in her mid- to late twenties, and wore a tight blue skirt, a white blouse, and high-heeled shoes that added three inches to her height. Her jewelry was simple, consisting of a small gold chain with a cross around her neck and an Apple watch on her left wrist. Guimond directed her to a chair at the conference table at the rear of his office, where she sat and crossed her legs.

In front of her was a three-page nondisclosure agreement indicating that whatever information she was provided, verbal or written, could not be discussed with anyone outside the police department unless she received written permission. Noel said that such agreements were standard in her business and signed it without reading beyond the first paragraph. The document below the NDA was the government's standard hourly rate contract for consultants. Apparently, she was also familiar with this, and after quickly looking at the two-page agreement, she signed it too.

Once these formalities were complete, Guimond went to his desk and brought over a laptop, the flash drive containing the Ritz camera data, and a second flash drive containing the email and attachments that the anonymous source had sent.

An hour after she'd started, Noel closed the cover of the laptop. Guimond, who had been working at his desk while Noel went through the materials, looked up as she handed him the laptop.

"There's no question that the camera data given to you by the Ritz has been altered. The notes and attachments on the second flash drive perfectly document the alterations that occurred."

"You're 100 percent certain?"

"Yes. It is irrefutable that the laws of geometry, mathematics, and physics were broken in creating a false video narrative. I'll send you my report tomorrow, but I believe you already have the essence of what I'm going to say in the email you received." She then asked for his email address and asked if she could keep the flash drives in order to reference them in her report. Guimond didn't have a problem with either request, and after she signed a hand receipt for the flash drives, Noel left his office.

Guimond had earlier told his supervisor that he believed it was time to take a very close look at Amo Voclain and, by extension, Gamal Al-Mutairi. Normally, getting information from Saudi Arabia on one of its citizens was as hard as getting the Turks and Greeks to agree on something—meaning that it was possible, but not in this lifetime. However, something that had happened two years ago, which Guimond had essentially forgotten about until now, changed that time frame.

The experience had begun when Guimond met Mumtaz Radwan, a Saudi financier and close confidant to the royal family, at a diplomatic function given for the Saudi Arabian minister of finance. Guimond, who was overseeing external security at the event on behalf of the French government, struck up a conversation with the financier when Guimond was taking a smoking break and Radwan approached and asked him for a light. Afterward, they exchanged business cards, their conversation having lasted no more than ten minutes.

Guimond would later learn from Radwan that the Saudi was in Paris because the minister of finance had asked him to quietly negotiate the purchase of a company. The reason he wanted Radwan and not his attorneys to do this was twofold. The first was that he didn't believe attorneys were good businessmen, and he wanted Radwan to negotiate the business portion of the transaction. The second was that the company would double its price if it suspected that a member of the royal family was the purchaser. With Radwan presenting himself as the purchaser, that fact could be hidden. After Radwan agreed, the minister had asked an additional favor—that Radwan pick up a matching necklace and bracelet that the minister had bought at Graaf Diamonds for his wife's birthday. Unfortunately, because he'd requested that additional diamonds be added to the set, neither item would be ready until the next day. Radwan readily agreed and said that he would bring the jewelry with him on his return flight to Riyadh, which was scheduled for the following evening.

The following day, Radwan picked up the jewelry without incident and took it back to his hotel room. Since his room safe was too small to hold the boxes containing the necklace and bracelet, he left them on the desk next to his briefcase. His intention was to place them in the hotel safe on the way to his meeting. However, as he would later explain to Guimond, his day began to fall apart when he received an unexpected call on a critical business matter that lasted much longer than he anticipated. This made him late for his meeting. When the call ended, he grabbed his briefcase with one hand and dialed his driver on his cell with the other as he ran from the room. It wasn't until he finished his meeting that he remembered that he'd left the jewelry on his desk.

When he returned to his hotel, both boxes were where he'd left them. However, upon opening them, he saw that the bracelet and necklace were gone. He couldn't file a police report because the theft would make the evening news. This would not only embarrass the minister but also destroy the trust the royal family had placed in him. He had enough money to buy replacements, even though, from what he knew, the value of the necklace and bracelet was over a million dollars. But the pieces would take time to replicate—and time was in short supply since he was scheduled to leave the country that night. That's when he remembered the card Capitaine Guimond had given him. Radwan phoned and asked for a private meeting, saying there was something important he needed to discuss, but he couldn't do it over the phone. When Guimond came to the hotel, Radwan told him everything.

Leaving Radwan's hotel room, Guimond went downstairs, showed his credentials to the manager, and asked for the keycard entry log to Radwan's room during the time the financier had said he was away. Guimond soon discovered that the only person who'd entered the room was a beverage service person who had checked the status of the minibar. Obtaining the name and address of this person, who lived two hours by bus outside the city, the captain got in his car and raced to the residence, arriving five minutes before the woman strode up the walk to her apartment building. Not bothering with formalities, he took the backpack off her shoulders and found the jewelry inside. Wanting to avoid the publicity that a report would generate, he told her to leave Paris within twenty-four hours or be arrested. The following day, she failed to report for work, and when Guimond checked her apartment, it was devoid of personal items. She'd taken him up on his offer.

Radwan was in tears when Guimond handed him the jewelry. Before he left for the airport, he made Guimond a promise: if the captain ever needed a favor, no matter what it was, Radwan would grant it. Today Guimond was going to take him up on that promise.

The call with the Saudi financier was all that Guimond had hoped it would be. Although Radwan was surprised by the request, he said that he'd make it happen. Three hours after they spoke, Guimond answered a call from a 966 prefix—Saudi Arabia.

"Since my inquiry, Gamal Al-Mutairi has attracted a great deal of attention," Radwan said without preamble. "It seems that his birth certificate indicates that he's seven years of age— or would have been if he hadn't died shortly after birth. The passport has now been revoked. It was issued by a government official who died two days after its issue. Because the man was apparently a great deal overweight, no one bothered to perform an autopsy. His coworkers attested that he'd had a bad case of flu, and that was listed as the cause of death. I'll give you the name of a government official whom you can reference to verify this information. I'll also email you the passport photo."

After the exchange of a few pleasantries, the call ended. Guimond was about to ask his superior to issue an arrest warrant for Gamal Al-Mutairi, or whoever he really was, when his desk phone rang. Amo Voclain was dead.

CHAPTER 8

T HE WRECK HAD been horrific and had occurred, according to a witness, when a car cut in front of a sixteen-wheeled gasoline truck, missing it by a breath in order to make an off-ramp that it had, for all practical purposes, passed. The driver of the eighty-thousand-pound, seventy-foot-long vehicle slammed on the truck's brakes to miss the car and lost control. Thankfully, the truck turned sharply to the right and plunged into a ditch to the side of the road, avoiding the other cars on the highway. Unfortunately, it veered into the exact spot where a Renault, for some unknown reason, had previously pulled off the road and stopped. The forty-ton truck crushed the car as if it were a grape, before consuming it in a massive fireball that shot thirty feet into the air. According to the witness, who'd pulled to the side of the highway and stopped, the truck's driver managed to survive by jumping out of his vehicle as it left the road.

Unsurprisingly, it was later learned that the driver of the Renault was crushed and incinerated within his vehicle. According to an EMS technician who later arrived, the remains within the Renault were in such poor shape that for all he knew, it could have been Elvis inside the car. Fortunately, the victim's wallet and passport, which the police theorized must have been on either the dash or the center console, were hurled through the open driver's window by the force of the explosion and survived the inferno. The driver's license identified the deceased as Amo Voclain. Five feet from the singed wallet and passport was an empty bottle of vodka, which also had been ejected from the vehicle. This led police to conclude that the driver of the Renault either was inebriated or had tried to pull off the highway to finish the vodka when the truck plowed into him. Either way, from the charred bones that had survived, the technicians estimated that the deceased had been approximately six feet seven, matching the height of the person on the driver's license.

Voclain's staged death didn't come cheaply. Following the incident, Rizzo wired a million dollars to an offshore account. The corpse, a man who had once played for an Italian basketball team before ultimately becoming a shoe salesman in a town outside Milan, had been spotted by one of the Unione Corse members tasked with finding a suitable body. The unfortunate substitute for Voclain was killed while taking out the trash, and his body was driven to the spot where he'd eventually be crushed and incinerated. The person who drove him there in the Renault wore gloves and placed the vodka bottle, wallet, and passport that Voclain had provided far enough away from the vehicle to not be destroyed. He also placed a tree branch on the side of the road to mark the spot where the truck should veer off the road. The drivers of the gasoline truck and the car that would swerve in front of it were in constant communication and orchestrated their near collision to perfection. Once the truck had crushed the Renault, the driver, who had leaped from the vehicle, pressed the button on a remote-control transmitter. This set off an explosive charge under the truck and detonated the gas. When the police arrived, the truck driver gave his statement, which was subsequently verified by a witness who'd stopped to help. He was then taken to a nearby hospital, where he voluntarily submitted to a blood test. With no alcohol or drugs in his system, he was driven home by the police.

Elia Donati walked out of jail looking haggard and disheveled, dressed in the dark blue jogging suit and athletic shoes that Bruno had brought to the prison. Bruno was waiting for him outside, and the two chief inspectors hugged. Standing near them were Guimond and Donais.

They drove to the Ritz and, thanks to Guimond's phone call to management, were escorted to the Coco Chanel suite, a 2,045-square-foot two-bedroom palatial accommodation that went for $30,000 per night. The manager told them they could stay there as long as they liked as the hotel's way of apologizing for what had happened as a result of someone hacking into their surveillance system and altering the video. The clothes and personal belongings that Donati and Bruno had left in their rooms had been neatly laundered or dry-cleaned and put away in the two-bed room that they would share. Donais had brought clothing and other items from her residence earlier in the day, which she placed in the other bedroom.

After the manager left, Donati excused himself. A few minutes later, the sound of the shower could be heard. While Donati was cleaning up, Bruno ordered a celebratory meal. Just as it arrived, a transformed Donati emerged from the bedroom, looking like an advertisement for *GQ* magazine. Although he still looked tired, he was dressed in a tan suit, a white shirt, and a light blue tie.

As they sat in the living room and poured themselves libations from one of the two bottles of Billecart-Salmon Brut Reserve champagne that accompanied their meal, Guimond brought everyone up-to-date on the report he'd received from Claudine Noel, on Voclain's death, and on the story of Gamal Al-Mutairi.

"I believe if you dig deep enough, you'll discover that Gamal Al-Mutairi and Cesare Rizzo are one and the same and that his offshore trust purchased his father's estate and assets in Bellagio," Bruno said.

"I have a photo of Gamal Al-Mutairi, but not one of Cesare Rizzo, although I've requested it from Rome. However, assuming you're right, I have no basis to charge him with anything other than entering the country illegally, a serious crime for which we'll start the process to deport him to Saudi Arabia. However, I'm not entirely convinced that effort will be successful."

"Why not?" Donais asked.

"We have to assume that he'll employ the best legal minds in France to cut a deal. He does have some leverage because of the real estate investments his trust has made in France. I did a computer search, and it seems that Rizzo, which I'll call him instead of Gamal Al-Mutairi, owns tens of millions of dollars in property. The government might care more about those investments and the taxes and the jobs they generate than the name on a passport. Believe me—the story he'll come up with as to why he used a false name and had a Saudi passport will be worthy of a Hollywood movie."

"Are you still moving forward with his deportation?"

"Assuming it isn't blocked, I'll have a court order to that effect in twenty-seven days," Guimond said. "Again, that's assuming his lawyers don't fight it and get a stay order."

"Why so long?" Donati asked.

"The law requires eight separate approvals, each with a mandatory three-day waiting period to allow for comments. I'm working with close friends who will give these approvals in the minimum amount of time and without comment, keeping the paperwork outside their bureaucracy so no one picks up the phone and calls Rizzo's attorneys or the media. Like it or not, he's a beneficiary of what's happening in France, with all the various nationalities migrating into our country, half of whom have no documentation whatsoever. Therefore, with his wealth and investments in France, and assuming his advisors give him a good excuse for having a false passport, I believe he'll get a sympathetic ear from the judge and be allowed to stay."

"Assuming the deportation process does succeed, what happens next?" Bruno asked.

"I go to his residence, serve the court order, and take him directly to the airport. I already have his ticket because the last thing I want is for the flight to Riyadh to be sold out when I arrive at the airport. Once I take him into custody, there won't be enough time for him to call a lawyer. When we land, I'll hand him over to the Mabahith, the Saudi secret police. They'll find out what is really going on because I don't believe they employ the same interrogative techniques we do."

"With Voclain dead, and Cesare Rizzo likely to be a guest of the Saudis for quite some time, I believe justice will be served," Bruno said.

Once they had finished their flutes of champagne, they started on the meal sent up from L'Espadon, one of the finest restaurants in Paris. They had no idea how much it cost because Bruno didn't even look at the check when he signed the manager's name in place of the room number.

Cesare Rizzo's first clue as to what was happening occurred the same day that Bruno, Donati, and Donais were escorted to their suite at the Ritz, when Air France phoned the number they had on file for Gamal Al-Mutairi. Rizzo had once used the airline for last-minute travel when his Gulfstream G650 was being serviced and a charter aircraft wasn't available. Apparently, the French carrier's computer system was astoundingly efficient because it recognized Gamal Al-Mutairi as someone who'd flown first-class in the past yet was sitting in economy for an upcoming flight to Saudi Arabia. The person who called wondered if Al-Mutairi wanted to upgrade, given that first-class seats were still available. Since Rizzo had not purchased a ticket, he asked the person calling if his travel agent, although he had none, had made the reservation. The response he received told him all he needed to know—the French government had purchased the seat on the 8:45 p.m. flight, four weeks from now. After declining to upgrade, he hung up.

Rizzo, who'd had an emergency departure plan ready the day he entered the country, required two phone calls to implement his plan. However, since he had a month before he was to be deported, he wanted to use that time to balance the books on those who'd caused him so much trouble.

CHAPTER 9

TWENTY-SEVEN DAYS LATER, with deportation order in hand, Guimond and another officer entered the courtyard of Rizzo's mansion in Saint-Germain-des-Prés. The residence looked abandoned, with the gate unexpectedly open and no vehicle visible in the courtyard. Making his way to the front door, with the other officer beside him, Guimond banged the brass knocker several times to announce their presence, noticing after the fact a security camera above the door and to their right. Upon seeing it, he took his credentials from his inside jacket pocket and held them up to the camera. Twenty seconds later, the door opened, and Guimond came face-to-face with Voclain. Stunned, he didn't see the gun that would take his life. The bullet made a small hole in his heart muscle when it entered and a bigger one when it exited. The officer to Guimond's right saw Voclain's gun and tried to draw his weapon from its holster. He never got that opportunity. Voclain's second shot found the center of his forehead.

Rizzo, who'd watched the killings on the camera monitor, arrived at the front door as two of his security staff were wrapping the bodies inside a tarp and securing it with tape so that the blood wouldn't escape onto the floor of the Range

Rover. The bodies would be left at the foot of the Paris Police Memorial in the Montparnasse Cemetery, where they were certain to be found. Rizzo had thought about having the Unione Corse dispose of them in the waters outside Marseille, but he had a great deal of respect for Guimond and his tenacity in exposing Gamal Al-Mutairi. He believed it a fitting tribute to place him in front of the memorial. In the end, the same tenacity that had made him a great inspector required that he die.

The mansion was virtually empty of the antiques, furniture, and artworks that had filled its interior less than a month ago. These items, along with the Maybach, had already been crated and taken away by the Unione Corse and were on their way to their destination. Rizzo and Voclain would depart Paris on his Gulfstream G650 from Le Bourget Airport, which was exclusively for the use of private aircraft, a twenty-five-minute ride from the residence. Rizzo looked around the residence that had been his home for the past seven years with a look of detachment. He was ready to leave. All that remained before that could happen was the placement of one last item.

The Gulfstream completed its five-thousand-mile journey in slightly less than ten hours, touching down at the Dzaoudzi–Pamandzi International Airport in Mayotte, an archipelago in the northern Mozambique Channel of the Indian Ocean, between Madagascar and northeastern Mozambique. Because it was part of France, no visas or special documents were required as Rizzo, followed by Voclain, disembarked the aircraft in a hangar at the far end of the 6,330-foot-long runway. There to greet them was Marcel Degos, a five-foot-five bundle of energy who was neither heavy nor thin, with closely cropped black hair covered by a ball cap bearing the *coq gaulois*, the logo of Les Bleus, the French national football team. He was wearing a short-sleeved open-collared white shirt, tan pants, and sunglasses. Standing behind him was a group of five white-suited workers who were there to paint the aircraft a different color and give it a new tail number.

Degos approached and introduced himself to Rizzo and Voclain, directing them to a nearby table, where Rizzo wordlessly set down the laptop he was carrying in his left hand and connected a satellite phone to its port. Sixty seconds later, Degos received the second half of his payment. Rizzo then handed him a debit card.

Their business concluded, Rizzo and Voclain were ushered into a waiting taxi, their trunks of personal items following in separate vehicles as Degos remained to oversee the change in identity of the aircraft.

Two days and two hours after the G650 landed in Mayotte, it set course for French Martinique, where it refueled before leaving for its next destination—the Motu Mute Airport off the island of Bora Bora in French Polynesia.

The person who found the body of Luc Guimond and the officer accompanying him was an eighty-year-old man who'd come to the Montparnasse Cemetery early in the morning to pay his respects to his late wife, who was buried not far from the memorial. It took an hour for the man, who desperately needed hip and knee replacement surgery, to find a groundskeeper and another thirty minutes for the cemetery employee to verify what the old man had seen and notify the police. As a result, it was nearly 11:00 a.m. when the first patrol car arrived. Once it was discovered that the bodies belonged to two police officers, a squadron of police vehicles arrived, soon followed by a horde of media. The officer in charge of this chaos was Superintendent Matthieu St. Amand. He knew of the romance between Guimond and Donais, and upon seeing that one of the officers was Guimond, he called Donais. By this time, she had moved back to her apartment and had invited Bruno and Donati to join her, all three agreeing that they'd imposed on the hospitality of the Ritz long enough.

When St. Amand informed Donais of Guimond's death, she fainted and collapsed to the floor. While Bruno carried her to the couch, Donati picked up the phone and spoke with St. Amand. When the conversation ended, he told Bruno what he'd learned.

Donais regained consciousness five minutes later, shivering despite the room being slightly on the warm side. Bruno went into her bedroom, found a blanket, and wrapped it around her before pouring a glass of orange juice and handing it to her. The tough private detective was inconsolable, irrationally chiding herself for not having accepted Guimond's proposal, feeling that if she had, this somehow would have prevented his death. It was Bruno who brought an end, at least for the moment, to Donais's self-chastisement.

"The only person to blame is the person who killed him, period," Bruno said. "I'm not going to say that your life hasn't changed and that you'll get over it, because both statements are utterly false. I can say emphatically from experience, since my wife and unborn child were murdered, that one never really gets over such trauma. You just learn to live with it. Take the best part of what Luc gave you and keep it close—that way he'll always be with you."

Bruno's revelation about the death of his wife and unborn child seemed to get both Donais and Donati's attention, their expressions becoming intent as they faced him more directly.

"That said, we go after who was responsible and bring them to justice—which is what Luc would have done if the situation were reversed."

That statement seemed to resonate well with Donais, who visibly began to calm down.

When Bruno finished speaking, Donati jumped in and relayed his conversation with St. Amand, who had said that preliminary evidence indicated that Guimond and the other officer weren't killed at the cemetery, but outside the front door of Rizzo's residence, where they had gone to serve a deportation order.

"I believe a good place to begin our search for Rizzo is at his residence," Bruno said, drawing agreement from Donati and Donais. "Maybe we can find a clue as to where he's gone."

When they arrived at the residence, they found the street cordoned off by police. Fortunately, Donais's relationship with Guimond was well known by fellow officers, and they let her, Bruno, and Donati through without so much as a question. After examining the blood splatters outside the front door, after which Donais ran to the bushes and threw up, they went inside and began looking around the mansion. Five minutes later, they came upon St. Amand, who didn't seem surprised to see them. He explained that his search was complete and that Rizzo, a.k.a. Gamal Al-Mutairi, had taken everything with him, except for a single framed photograph on the floor of his office and, next to the photo, three glasses and a partial bottle of Hennessy Beauté du Siécle Grand Champagne cognac.

Bruno asked if they could see the office, and St. Amand escorted them there.

"An airplane?" Donais said, picking up the photograph.

"A seventy-million-dollar Gulfstream G650," Donati replied. "The company my father works for has one. He says that it has a range of around eight thousand miles."

"I didn't know Rizzo had a plane," Donais said.

"I'm willing to bet that it belonged to his father and that he acquired it as part of his purchase of the estate through his offshore trust."

"Why leave this?" Donais asked.

"It's an invitation—and a taunt," Bruno replied. "He's saying, 'I'm no longer in Paris and could be anywhere in the world. Try and find me.' I'm betting that the cognac is his way of giving the three of us the middle finger and asking that we toast him because he outsmarted us and escaped."

"It was an expensive gesture," Donati said, showing Bruno his cell phone, where he'd googled the price of this particular cognac and found a bottle that was for sale for $300,000. "His immense wealth will make him hard to find," Donati said.

"Perhaps not as hard as you think," Donais replied, before walking away from Bruno and Donati and making several calls. Ten minutes later, she rejoined them. "I asked the Civil Aviation Authority if they could locate the aircraft, given that it would have had to file a flight plan. They said that they could, if I could provide the aircraft identification number. Unfortunately, this photo doesn't show a tail number." Turning to Bruno, she said, "I'm sure you can get that information from someone in Italy. As you said, it's probably his father's aircraft."

"It will take time, especially since we've just recently been cleared of murder charges and the rank and file within the state police may not fully trust us yet," Bruno replied.

"Maybe there's another approach," Donati said. "We just look at the flight plans of all Gulfstream G650s that left Paris shortly after Guimond's murder."

"That's doable," St. Amand replied, "since all private jets use Le Bourget Airport."

It would turn out to be anything but doable.

Working from Donais's apartment it took almost two days to recover the flight plans for aircraft flying out of Le Bourget Airport within six hours of Guimond's murder, since these aircraft had completed their flights without incident, and thus the data was now considered historical and stored in an archival system outside the airport's control. When the records were finally received, there was no flight plan filed for a G650 aircraft out of Le Bourget Airport in the time frame requested. That left everyone in agreement that Rizzo had left a photo of the Gulfstream as a red herring, a clue meant to mislead or distract. However, that belief quickly changed later in the day, when one of the tower staff, who had been on a two-day break, returned and heard about the police inquiry. She'd been on duty when a Gulfstream aircraft took off VFR, which meant that it didn't require a flight plan so long as it adhered to visual flight rules. The controller handling the aircraft said that she'd never seen a jet, especially one of this size, want to fly visually rather than by instruments because, after all, what was the point of having this type of aircraft if one was going to fly low and slow?

"It seems that Rizzo has left us with three possibilities," St. Amand said, refilling his coffee cup from the carafe on the table beside him. "The first is that he flew to an airport, likely somewhere in Europe, that the pilot could get to visually. The second is that the pilot flew by instruments anyway, at his normal altitude and speed, to his destination, which I have been told is unlikely since he would have been picked up on radar and reported as an unknown aircraft—something taken very seriously in this day and age. The third, and I'm told the most likely, possibility is that the pilot took off VFR and then filed a flight plan to his destination once he was en route."

"Then how do we sort this out?" Bruno asked.

St. Amand's suggestion was that they get an expert in air traffic control procedures to tell them how they would avoid detection if they had to escape in a private jet. He compared the group's current efforts to someone trying to solve a crime when his skill set was engineering instead of law enforcement. What they were trying to accomplish on their own, although possible, was unlikely.

St. Amand got the name and phone number of the person at Le Bourget who had worked the Gulfstream when it took off VFR. Reaching her by phone, St. Amand asked the controller how a private jet could avoid detection upon leaving an airfield. After thinking about it for less than thirty seconds, the controller responded that she would keep the Gulfstream's speed slow and its altitude low so that it wouldn't stand out from other aircraft flying in uncontrolled airspace, where air traffic control services are not deemed necessary. Therefore, a radar operator would automatically assume that the G650 was just another prop plane flying VFR. However, once the Gulfstream was within range of Belgium, which shared a border with France, the pilot could file a flight plan. Germany and Great Britain were also possible entry points into the air traffic control system through which a flight plan could be filed, but according to the controller, they tended to be more stringent on security and to ask more questions, and this would be the case especially with a Gulfstream.

Placing a call to the Belgian Civil Aviation Authority, St. Amand learned that a Gulfstream G650, traveling VFR within France, had initiated an IFR flight plan as it approached the Belgium border. The official gave him the tail number and the plane's destination, which St. Amand asked the official to repeat to ensure he'd heard correctly, the inflection in his voice indicating that he didn't quite believe what he was being told. Once he verified the destination, he ended the call.

"Rizzo's aircraft flew to the Dzaoudzi–Pamandzi International Airport in Mayotte," St. Amand said to Bruno, Donati, and Donais, who had been sitting near him during the conversation.

"That's not much of an escape," Donais said. "It's a part of France."

Bruno and Donati gave each other slightly confused looks, indicating that they had no idea where Mayotte was.

St. Amand seemingly picked up on this and explained. "Mayotte is an archipelago about 190 miles northwest of Madagascar, which is off the east coast of Africa. Distance-wise, it's approximately five thousand miles from Paris. And Mademoiselle Donais is correct—anyone there is subject to French law."

"We're missing something," Bruno said, looking at his cell phone, where he searched for Mayotte on Wikipedia. "First, I can't see someone who just killed two French police officers and who has Rizzo's resources hiding in any jurisdiction that is subject to French law. And second, Mayotte's economy is largely based on agriculture, fishing, and livestock. This hardly sounds like a place where Rizzo, who owns a seventy-million-dollar jet and drinks three-hundred-thousand-dollar bottles of cognac, would live."

"You're probably correct. But even if it's an intermediate stop on the way to his final destination, it doesn't matter," said St. Amand. "If he's on Mayotte, we can arrest him and bring him back to Paris. Let me phone my counterpart in Mayotte and see what he can tell me."

St. Amand called his office and got a contact name and phone number from his assistant. Upon reaching his counterpart in Mayotte, he asked him to check and see if Rizzo and his aircraft were still there. Two hours later, the Mayotte officer called back. St. Amand listened, took notes, and hung up five minutes later. His face, which was devoid of emotion, gave no clue as to what he'd heard.

"Rizzo's Gulfstream did land in Mayotte three days ago, but my counterpart believes that its tail number was changed since another G650, with a different number, took off two days after Rizzo's jet landed. Because only one G650 has touched down at that airport in the past six months, he believes the aircraft are one and the same. The good news is that I have that tail number."

"Can we trace the Gulfstream after it left Mayotte?" Bruno asked.

"We should be able to now that we have the new tail number."

St. Amand again phoned his office, this time asking for the number of the police liaison at the French Civil Aviation Authority. Once he reached that liaison, he gave her a snapshot of what he was looking for. She was extremely efficient, as it turned out, and after a few clicks of the keyboard, she informed him that a Gulfstream G650 with the tail number he'd given her was in flight to Martinique.

"That's also part of France," Donais said. "Another refueling point?"

"Perhaps," St. Amand answered. "Going from one French region to another is a smart move on Rizzo's part since he doesn't have to present a passport, only a national ID card. Therefore, if he's created a false identity, which I'm sure he has, he won't have to reveal it till he gets to where he's going."

"But since we have the tail number of his plane, we'll know where that is," Donais said.

"You would think. Somehow, I believe that Rizzo has more surprises in store for us. Let me make a phone call."

St. Amand phoned his counterpart at the Martinique police department and asked him to detain the Gulfstream. Minutes later, however, he received a call back telling him that that there was no aircraft with that tail number at the Martinique Aimé Césaire International Airport. However, a G650 with a different tail number had just departed for the Bora Bora Airport, located on the islet of Motu Mute in French Polynesia. After the Martinique officer gave St. Amand the tail number, the call ended.

St. Amand told Bruno that if he could, he'd order a French fighter to blow the Gulfstream out of the sky. He was tired of copying down tail numbers and being one step behind Rizzo. However, this destination gave them an advantage since the distance between the two islands was 6,557 miles. That meant that the French Civil Aviation Authority would be able to monitor the aircraft along its route to ensure it didn't change its destination. It also meant that they'd have someone waiting for the aircraft.

St. Amand's conversation with the police chief in Bora Bora was short. Not a lot more needed to be said once the chief learned that the man headed to the islet of Motu Mute was a cop killer. The chief made it clear that he'd coordinate a welcoming committee for the aircraft and that whoever was on board would have zero chance of escape.

The runway at the Bora Bora Airport on the islet of Motu Mute was made of asphalt and was 4,921 feet long. This was far too short for most passenger jets, so commercial traffic to the island utilized two-engine turboprop aircraft. Larger planes, both public and private, landed at Papeete on the main island of Tahiti, a fifty-minute flight away, where passengers transferred to the smaller turboprops.

Hearing that a Gulfstream had called in to the Bora Bora Airport and was on approach, ground personnel dropped what they were doing and gathered at the base of the small tower. Passengers who were awaiting the departure of their aircraft noticed this and, curious as to what was going on, began to congregate near the terminal's window. Therefore, the entire airport was watching as the large Gulfstream G650 set down on the micro-runway. The instant the wheels hit the asphalt, the pilot activated his reverse thrusters, speed brakes, and foot brakes. He would have thrown out an anchor if he'd had one to ensure the aircraft stopped before it reached the end of the runway, after which it would have needed pontoons and a maritime certificate. As it turned out, the aircraft stopped two hundred feet short of needing that certification.

After the pilot taxied to the terminal, shut down both engines, and extended the passenger ramp, four officers rushed onboard, guns drawn. While one of them remained at the front of the plane and told the pilots to stay in the cockpit, the other three raced to the rear of the plane, where the aircraft's sole passenger was nonchalantly smoking a cigar and sitting at a teak desk. Upon seeing the officers, he set the cigar on a silver tray, stood, and interlocked his fingers atop his head.

CHAPTER 10

S T. AMAND PERSONALLY delivered the news to Bruno, Donati, and Donais that the sole passenger aboard the Gulfstream that had landed in Bora Bora had been taken into custody. Although his passport was not that of Cesare Rizzo or Gamal Al-Mutairi, St. Amand said that he hadn't expected either of those two names to be used by Rizzo since he was wanted for murder under both identities. Unfortunately, the superintendent continued, the subject of Rizzo's return was a matter of intense internal discussion—not regarding whether he should be extradited back to France, but regarding who should pay for it. He went onto explain that the Inspectorate General didn't want to expend the funds necessary to buy a ticket for one of its officers to escort Rizzo back to Paris, especially when the Ministry of Justice was administratively tasked with returning him. Since both departments' budgets were tight, neither wanted to cough up the money. Therefore, there was no telling how long resolution of this internal disagreement could take. On the other hand, St. Amand said, looking coyly at no one in particular, if the three of them bought their own tickets and wanted to pick up Rizzo and escort him back to Paris for trial, that would significantly expedite the process. To complete the legalities, he'd swear in Donais, a French citizen, as a police officer and give her a badge.

Bruno and Donais had limited savings, but both quickly said that they'd have no problem with that plan. Donati, who came from a wealthy family and could probably buy a house with his American Express Centurion Card, quickly said their contributions wouldn't be necessary. He gallantly absorbed the cost of all three tickets, which turned out to be extremely expensive since they were purchased at the last minute. Once the transportation issue was resolved, St. Amand gave Donais the folder he'd been carrying, which contained the paperwork necessary to arrest and transport Cesare Rizzo, alias Gamal Al-Mutairi, back to Paris. He said that he'd already emailed copies of the documents to David Bascou, the chief of police in Bora Bora.

Two hours later, Bruno, Donati, and Donais were boarding their aircraft.

The flight from Paris to Bora Bora required three connections and took thirty-five hours and twenty-five minutes. Bruno, Donati, and Donais, sleep-deprived prior to the flight, took this opportunity to get some rest. The remainder of the time, they spent in a state of anxiety, hoping the elusive scion wouldn't lawyer his way out of police custody and leave before they arrived.

A day and a half after they left Paris, they deplaned the twin-engine prop on Motu Mute and walked toward the small terminal, each with a carry-on bag slung over their shoulder. Halfway there, they were intercepted by Chief Bascou, who held photos of each of them in his hand. After introducing himself, he asked if they'd like to inspect the Gulfstream before seeing Rizzo. When all three indicated that they would, he escorted them toward the aircraft, which wasn't hard to spot since it was parked thirty yards away and cordoned off with yellow police tape.

After one of the ground crew lowered the stairway and turned on the internal aircraft lighting, the group boarded.

"We searched the aircraft quite thoroughly," Bascou said. "There was no contraband on this plane."

"Are there any documents, computers, iPads—anything that can give us an insight into his activities?" Bruno asked.

"None of those, I'm afraid. The only electronic device we found was his cell phone, which we couldn't access because it's password-protected."

They continued toward the back of the aircraft, where Bruno stopped and looked down at the cigar resting on a silver tray. Beside it was an empty bottle of 1959 Dom Perignon, along with a depleted tin of Almas caviar and a small silver spoon. "This looks like Rizzo's style," Donati said.

"The refrigerator on this aircraft is quite large and has a case of champagne and a dozen more tins of caviar inside."

"I've seen enough," Bruno said, receiving concurring nods from Donati and Donais. "Let's go see Rizzo."

Bascou led them to a police boat, which was moored behind the terminal, and they set off for Vaitape, the largest city on the island of Bora Bora, with a population of 4,927.

It took fifteen minutes to make the four-and-a-half-mile crossing. The police building, a single-story light yellow rectangular cement-block structure, was not far from where they docked. When they arrived, Bruno, Donati, and Donais were taken to the interrogation room while Bascou went to get Rizzo. Prior to leaving Paris, Donais had asked St. Amand for Guimond's handcuffs. She now held them in her hand as she waited for Rizzo to enter.

Five minutes later, Bascou returned with his prisoner.

"That's not him," Donais said as Bascou escorted the man to a plastic chair behind a rectangular metal table, both of which were anchored to the floor.

"This was the only passenger on board the Gulfstream. Although the name on the passport he was carrying was not Cesare Rizzo or Gamal Al-Mutairi, your superintendent told me that this person would probably be using an alias. The only things he had on him were a debit card from an overseas bank, a passport, and a national ID card in the name of Marcel Degos. I believe he was expecting you because when I asked if he wanted an attorney, he said—"

"I said," Degos interrupted, "that I didn't want to call my attorney in Papeete until my Parisian visitors arrived."

"What's your story?" Bruno asked. "Who are you?"

"As my passport shows, I'm Marcel Degos. As to my story, that's immaterial since I've done nothing illegal."

"What about changing the tail numbers on the Gulfstream?" Donati asked.

"Those changes were legally processed and registered with the appropriate agencies by my attorneys. Therefore, no laws have been broken."

"And I suppose you don't know the owner," Bruno said.

"I never met him. I just spoke with him on the phone. He asked me to do him a favor and take his aircraft to Bora Bora, and I obliged. Who wouldn't want to come here on a private jet, all expenses paid?"

"As impossible as that is to believe, let me ask you another question," Bruno said. "Do you know Cesare Rizzo, alias Gamal Al-Mutairi?"

"I've never heard of either."

"I think you have," Donais said.

"Prove it."

Bascou handcuffed Degos to the interrogation room table and nodded for Bruno, Donati, and Donais to follow him outside.

He closed the door behind them and moved to a spot away from the door where Degos couldn't hear them. "I have to release him. He's broken no law, and there's no warrant for his arrest." Receiving no disagreement, Bascou went back inside the interrogation room to tell Degos that he was setting him free.

"We've been set up," Bruno said to Donati and Donais. "While we've been chasing the Gulfstream, Rizzo escaped. Given that he's had days to get to his secure hiding place, we'll be lucky to find him now."

"What now?" Donais asked.

"I would normally say that we should stay and enjoy the splendid scenery," said Donati, "but I'm not in the mood, and I suspect that neither of you are either. We still have seats on the return flight. The fact is, the longer we're away, the harder it will be to find Rizzo."

Just then, Bascou escorted Degas, minus his handcuffs, out of the interrogation room. As Degas was walking past Bruno, he suddenly stopped. Pulling Bruno toward him, he whispered something in his ear before Bascou yanked him away. The chief then took his soon-to-be-released prisoner down the hall to send him on his way.

"What was that about?" Donati asked.

"There's one more thing that we have to do before we go back to Paris," Bruno responded, explaining to Donati and Donais what he meant as they walked toward the building exit.

The police boat took them back to the airport. At Bruno's request, Bascou was allowing them to search the G650 one more time before they boarded their aircraft.

"What did he say again?" Donati asked.

"Press the button under the desk on the plane," Bruno said as they walked to the rear of the aircraft.

"Which does what?" Donati asked.

"I don't know, but I have a guess. Do you remember how Rizzo choreographed that scene in his mansion—with the cognac and the photo of this aircraft?"

"How could I forget? I agree with what you said then," Donais replied. "He was giving us the finger."

"He wanted us to toast his brilliance and the fact that he'd outwitted us with an extraordinarily expensive cognac. I believe we got that part right. However, we also believed that he was taunting us with a photo of an aircraft that we previously hadn't known he had. Now we know that the photo of the plane was there so that we'd chase it halfway around the world while he escaped."

"And?" Donais asked.

"And he knew that we'd all end up here, chasing a passenger on his aircraft while he went to ground. Rizzo is an egomaniac and a narcissist. I believe that he wanted to boast about how he outwitted the three of us again. But he couldn't be as obvious as before because of the scenario he created. Whatever message he left, he wanted it to be for our eyes only."

"And you believe Degas was telling you how to find that message," Donati said.

"I'm certain of it," Bruno replied.

It was Donais who found the release button that Degas had referred to, hidden in an unobtrusive recess under the desktop. When pressed, it opened a secret compartment in the wooden floor under the teak desk. The space itself was square, one foot to a side, and contained a single sheet of heavy linen paper. Donais removed it and turned the paper toward the light from the cabin window.

Written in black ink with a fountain pen, in a strong and confident hand, was Rizzo's message:

> "Abandonner est toujours une option, mais pas toujours un échec." — Cameron Conaway, *En cage: Mémoires d'un poète de la cage-fighting*

Translated, the quote said, "Giving up is always an option, but not always a failure."

CHAPTER 11

LORENZO SPADA, A.K.A. Gamal Al-Mutairi, a.k.a. Cesare Rizzo, was enjoying a Hennessy Beauté du Siécle Grand Champagne cognac, intermittently puffing from his Cohiba 1966 Edicion Limitada 2011 cigar between sips. The execution of his departure from Paris had begun weeks ago, after the inquiry from Air France regarding an upgrade on the upcoming flight to Riyadh—which he didn't make. Knowledge of that date, later confirmed with a bribe paid to a Ministry of Justice official who notified Rizzo when the deportation order was issued, had allowed him to orchestrate his escape, the activation of which had required two calls. The first had been to his expediter, who coordinated the transport of his household goods and his departure from Paris, and the second had been to the Union Corse. Following these calls, a packing company had arrived and crated furniture, paintings, antiques, and other valuables. Personal items such as clothing were placed in trunks and sent ahead to the Gulfstream and loaded in the cargo compartment and on board the aircraft. The last touch, planting a photograph of his Gulfstream and a partial bottle of cognac, had been critical to his escape in that it had led his pursuers away from Rizzo's new home.

Whether it was luck, good detective work, or a combination of both, Rizzo believed that the three investigators who'd been nipping at his heels were formidable and, if left unaddressed, would eventually expose him. The discovery of his Saudi passport was illustrative of this tenacity. Therefore, his escape plan, which had been in place since the day he arrived in Paris, needed to be modified. He had subsequently notified his expeditor that he wanted to add what he referred to as crumbs and an accelerant to the fire he would be creating by fleeing Paris. However, these investigators had to believe that they'd discovered their clues through superior detective work and that as a result they were closing in on their prey undetected, when in fact they were following a bread-crumb trail. The expeditor agreed to the changes, and the clues and misinformation were added to the already complex departure scenario.

Leaving Paris by visual flight rules and initiating a flight plan outside Belgium had been one of those crumbs. An average detective would have had a difficult, possibly unsuccessful, time uncovering this subtlety. But Rizzo wasn't dealing with average, and the three investigators who were pursuing him didn't disappoint when they eventually traced the aircraft to Mayotte, much faster than anticipated. Rizzo was thankful he hadn't gone with the original escape plan, which had called for flying his plane to Belgium and, while over Brussels, changing his destination to Mayotte. The accelerant had been the act of giving the aircraft a new tail number and paint job, causing the three investigators to believe they'd outsmarted him and were tracking his aircraft in spite of his efforts to throw them off. Martinique was a required fuel stop and had always been the second destination, chosen because it was a French region that didn't require a passport if the person entering was a French citizen. No crumb was needed, only an accelerant, which again was changing the tail number. By the time the aircraft reached Bora Bora, the only thing required to end the charade was Bruno, Donati, and Donais's presence.

Rizzo was sitting in a particularly comfortable chair and looking out over the marina. His seventieth-floor penthouse provided a magnificent view of the setting sun as it spread a pale tint of orange across the horizon. This view had not come cheap. His 25,000-square-foot condominium, which comprised the top two floors of the building, had cost $150 million, an amount that didn't faze him because his investments and entrepreneurial thievery alone generated more than this each year. He had selected this new domicile not only for its view but also because the building's security was stringent. That meant he didn't have to rely solely on Voclain—correction, Fabiano Tanzi—for his safety.

His new home had all the creature comforts he could desire, save one: a Mercedes Maybach Pullman Guard. With its heavy body and floor armor, blast-resistant windows, and ultra-luxurious interior, he felt both bathed in luxury and safe in its protective shell. The Rolls-Royce Phantom in which Voclain was currently chauffeuring him was extremely luxurious, but it wasn't the cocoon he wanted. The good news was that it wouldn't be long before the Maybach arrived, and he'd once again experience the peace it gave him.

Rizzo placed his cigar on the small silver tray beside him and poured himself another cognac. He still held a grudge against Bruno and Donati for what they'd done to his father and his family name. Their imprisonment would have balanced the scales of justice, allowing him to focus on expanding his financial empire and finding himself a bride to continue the family name. What he needed to do now was try to address this imbalance—and he knew exactly how to do it.

If the thirty-five-hour, twenty-five-minute three-connection flight to Bora Bora had seemed long, the return flight, which was an hour shorter, seemed interminable because they'd come back empty-handed. Bruno, Donati, and Donais slept little, preferring instead to try to figure out where Rizzo had gone. But when the plane landed a day and a half later, they were still at square one.

They went to Donais's residence. After they showered and put on fresh clothes, they found themselves famished, having eaten only airline food for the past three days. Bruno, who was a good cook, looked inside Donais's refrigerator and, finding eggs, butter, and some vegetables, cooked three omelets while Donati made espressos. None of them had much to say as they ate; the length of the flights and the disappointment over not finding Rizzo had drained their physical and emotional energy. After cleaning the kitchen, they went as a group into Donais's living room, and all three crashed on the couch. Bruno and Donati were half-asleep when someone knocked at the door. Donais, who knew it was St. Amand because he'd called earlier to say he was coming by, opened the door and let him in.

"I'm sorry this didn't turn out the way we expected," St. Amand said, kissing Donais on both cheeks.

Bruno and Donati approached and shook hands with the superintendent. Donais motioned for St. Amand to sit on the couch next to Donati, while she and Bruno sat in chairs adjacent to it.

"Don't be unnecessarily hard on yourself," St. Amand began. "No one knew that Cesare Rizzo wasn't on the aircraft that landed in Bora Bora. There was no way for you to know that he'd gotten Marcel Degos to take his place."

"Nevertheless, he's in the wind," Donais replied.

"Not necessarily," St. Amand responded, removing two thick folders from the black ballistic nylon briefcase he'd brought with him. He handed both folders to Donais. "The top folder contains a list of everyone who left Mayotte within forty-eight hours of the Gulfstream's departure. The bottom contains the names of everyone who left Martinique within forty-eight hours of the Gulfstream's arrival," St. Amand said. "Gamal Al-Mutairi and Amo Voclain both checked into the Emperor Hotel in Mayotte not long after Rizzo's Gulfstream landed. They've since checked out and left. But the island isn't big, and outsiders get noticed. My counterpart has assured me they're gone."

"Back up. You're saying that Voclain is alive?" Bruno asked, expressing the same disbelief that was visible on the faces of Donati and Donais.

"The owner of the hotel told the police," St. Amand said, removing a small notebook from his jacket pocket and flipping through several pages before he got to the one he wanted, "that a large man, approximately six feet, seven inches in height and wearing cowboy boots, with a neck that looked like a tree trunk, was accompanying a tall lanky man with legs that seemed too long for his body. This sounds like a description of Voclain and Rizzo to me."

"It does indeed," Bruno agreed.

"I should have known that Voclain wasn't killed in that tanker truck accident," said St. Amand. "How stupid it seems now to accept that his identification was miraculously flicked out the window of the car moments before thousands of gallons of fuel burned or melted everything else in the area.

Rizzo must have gone to quite a bit of trouble and expense to stage his death, which I'm guessing came as a result of the altercation Voclain had with the two of you"—St. Amand nodded at Donais and Bruno—"and Guimond."

"We all naively accepted it, because we wanted it to be true," Donais added.

"Spilled milk," Bruno replied. "They won't get away from us a second time. What would you like us to do, Superintendent?"

"Keep working the case. I don't know if Rizzo has informants within the department, but given his wealth, let's make that assumption. Therefore, if you discover anything, report it only to me."

St. Amand was silent for a moment before he spoke again. "My staff has checked the national ID and passport photograph, as well as the background, of everyone whose name is in those folders. None are Rizzo or Voclain. Frankly, I'm getting nowhere—which is why I need your investigative skills to ferret out clues that will lead us to this killer."

"If we're going to do this, it'd be useful to retain my police officer commission," Donais said.

"Keep it for now. I'll handle the blowback—if there is any."

"One other thing," Bruno said. "Chief Inspector Donati and I will need to speak with our superiors and request a leave of absence, so that we can stay in Paris and work on this with Lisette. I'm sure they'll give us the time off if you ask them."

"I'm positive they will," St. Amand responded, "because you both were fired two days ago—with a loss of pension and benefits, I might add. I was asked to pass this information on to you. I tried to intervene on both your behalves, but it doesn't seem that Italians take advice from the French in a very constructive manner. In fact, I believe I accelerated your demise. The Polizia di Stato is currently investigating the both of you because they don't concur with our computer expert's report that the Ritz video was altered. They need an independent analysis in order to make that determination."

"Send them the video," Donati said.

"I can't. It's a chain of custody thing. I can't send it to Italy because any competent defense attorney would say that the Polizia di Stato tampered with the video to protect the both of you. They're also not willing to accept a copy, even from my department. Therefore, I've invited them to view it here, and they've accepted."

"And that's all?" Donati asked, apparently picking up on something in St. Amand's demeanor that indicated there was more.

"There's also an internal investigation into the thirty kilos of heroin that was found in your car," St. Amand answered. "And since you and Chief Inspector Bruno are known to be friends, they're looking at the possibility of his involvement. Therefore, you're both unemployed until both these issues are resolved."

"Then I guess we have the time to go after Rizzo and Voclain," Bruno said, "as long as you don't mind them returning to France in body bags."

"I'll leave the logistics of their return up to you."

CHAPTER 12

RIZZO WATCHED ON the LCD security screen in his study as the Corsican entered the building and passed through the various layers of security before being allowed entry into a specific elevator. There were no buttons inside, and the doors silently closed once the visitor entered. The elevator quickly took him to the seventieth-floor penthouse.

The man who stepped off the elevator and into Rizzo's foyer was thirty years old and five feet, ten inches tall. He had a broad chest, black curly hair, and light stubble across his face, even though he'd apparently shaved not long ago. He wore black slacks and a matching long-sleeved shirt. The visitor had many names but had been born Antone Petru. He was the Unione Corse's premier assassin, and his services were not cheap, with his employer charging $125,000 per hit and providing a guarantee that the target would be killed, even if circumstances out of their control necessitated re-engaging the target.

As Petru approached Rizzo, he made eye contact with Voclain, who stood between them holding a silenced handgun at his side. If that bothered Petru, his facial expression didn't reflect it, and Rizzo directed him to a chair beside his, which had a commanding view of the marina. Voclain took his position five paces behind them.

"The reason you're here is to take possession of this," Rizzo said, forgoing pleasantries and getting straight to the point. He opened a drawer in the table next to his chair and removed a walnut case containing the gold-plated Beretta Px4 Storm Deluxe semiautomatic pistol that his father had used to kill himself and that Cesare Rizzo had acquired as part of the asset purchase of his estate. "I want you to use this gun to kill these two men. I believe they're in Paris, but if not, you'll have to find them." Rizzo handed Petru photos of Bruno and Donati, which had been stored inside the gun case.

The assassin carefully looked at the two faces before folding the photos and putting them in his back pocket. Petru, who didn't seem to be a conversationalist, nodded his acceptance of what he'd been told. Their business concluded, the assassin got up and, without uttering a word, began walking back to the elevator, carrying the walnut case in his left hand. Voclain, who still carried the silenced handgun at his side, escorted him to the foyer, staying several paces behind the assassin.

Just as Petru reached the elevator, he turned and, in a lighting-fast move, drew a ceramic knife from under his left shirt sleeve and hurled it toward Voclain. The look of surprise on Voclain's face was followed by one of relief when the knife tore into the collar of his jacket, effectively pinning him to the elegant wood paneling behind him. It all happened so quickly that he didn't have time to lift his gun hand.

Petru continued to show no emotion. He had undoubtedly thrown the knife to make the point that he was the alpha assassin in the room and could kill Voclain anytime he wanted. Pressing the elevator button, he waited a moment for the doors to open and then stepped inside as Voclain, unable to pull out the knife, which was buried deep in the wood, began to remove his jacket to dislodge himself.

Bruno, Donati, and Donais had spent the last five hours poring over the information given to them by St. Amand. In the end, sore backs and an increasing amount of frustration were all they had to show for their efforts.

"I have a question," Donais said. "Why change the aircraft color? That had to take time."

"My guess is that Rizzo's plane had an exceptional paint job," Bruno answered, "one that would generate envy. That would be in keeping with his narcissistic tendencies and desire to display his great wealth. Repainting it and changing the tail number was an attempt to throw anyone chasing him off the trail because the aircraft would appear to belong to a different owner."

"That said, two six-and-a-half-foot-tall men traveling together are not inconspicuous," said Donais. "Furthermore, judging from the cognac he left, Rizzo is the type of person who's accustomed to luxury—be it clothes, transportation, food, or whatever. He'd stand out from the crowd just because of who he is."

"Maybe we're coming at this the wrong way," Bruno said, running his hands through his hair as he leaned back in his chair and let out a frustrated sigh. "Let's put ourselves in Rizzo's place. We know from St. Amand that the police matched every nonresident who entered Mayotte with records of people who left or remained, beginning one day after Rizzo's arrival and ending the day his Gulfstream departed for Martinique. In doing this, they relied on the manifests required of public and private aircraft and marine vessels.

The manifest from the Gulfstream showed that both Rizzo and Voclain were on that aircraft, having used their real names. Hotel records show that they stayed at a local hotel for two days. However, after that they seem to have disappeared since there's no record of them leaving Mayotte. Knowing that, if you were Rizzo and wanted to leave undetected, how would you do it?" Bruno directed this last question to Donati.

Donati thought for nearly a minute before answering. "The first thing I'd do is disable or avoid the camera system at my point of departure so that there wouldn't be a visual record of my leaving."

"That box seems to have been checked, according to St. Amand. Private aircraft tend to arrive and depart from one of two aircraft hangars, neither of which has a security camera. The commercial arrival and departure terminals for both aviation and marine transports have security cameras. However, if there are no incidents, or no one requests a copy of the video, then the system overwrites itself every other day," Bruno replied. "Therefore, in line with what you said, Rizzo could have left Mayotte on a private or commercial aircraft or vessel without being recorded. What's the second thing you'd do?"

"I'd change my identity—passport, driver's license, and national ID card."

Bruno leaned forward and snapped his fingers. "A French citizen can go from one region of France to another, even though they're half a world apart, and no passport is required."

"Which is why the Gulfstream flew to Martinique," Donais interjected. "That meant that Degos wouldn't have to present a passport. His national ID card was good enough, and since the Gulfstream was only refueling and he didn't leave the plane, there was no manifest—only a note that one person was aboard."

"I think Rizzo had another reason for sending Degos to Martinique," Bruno said, lightly putting his fingers together in a steeple.

"Which was?" Donais asked.

"Once we tracked Degos there, Rizzo believed we wouldn't give Martinique a second thought, and that was a necessity."

"Why?" Donati asked.

Bruno explained his theory, including what needed to be done to prove it.

Once everyone was focused on Martinique, it took less than half an hour to find out how Rizzo and Voclain had left. In a comparison of the list of people who had departed Mayotte with those who had departed Martinique, two names stood out—Patric Beaufort and Damien Lowell. Both had boarded a commercial flight in Mayotte and also, miraculously, an hour later boarded an Air France flight in Martinique for Paris.

"This was a big mistake on Rizzo's part," Donati said.

"It was," Bruno agreed. "He didn't believe that we'd compare the passenger lists from both regions. Instead, he anticipated that we'd look only at the background information and photos of the people on the Mayotte manifests. In fact, he was counting on it because he wanted us to come to a dead end and eventually stop searching for him. This subterfuge was planned well before Rizzo and Voclain set foot in Mayotte. Beaufort and Lowell must have been contracted to hand over their passports so that they could be duplicated with Rizzo and Voclain's photos and then to travel to Mayotte and return to Paris by way of Martinique.

"Then Beaufort and Lowell managed to leave Mayotte twice—once to go to Martinique and once with Rizzo and Voclain assuming their identities."

"My guess is that they left not long after Rizzo landed, while he was staying at the hotel. If we look at earlier manifests, we should see their departure for Martinique."

Donati and Donais looked, and now that they knew what names they were searching for, they found that Beaufort and Lowell left for Martinique not long after Rizzo's arrival, just as Bruno had said.

"And now we trace Beaufort and Lowell from Mayotte," Donais said.

"That's exactly what we do," Bruno confirmed.

Using the police access codes that St. Amand had given her, Donais was able to access the airline's passenger lists. It didn't take long to discover Rizzo and Voclain's destination, which turned out to be Beirut, Lebanon.

"Very smart," Bruno said upon learning where they had gone. How he said those two words indicated that tracking them from Lebanon would be difficult, if not impossible. "I need a walk to clear my head."

"St. Amand said that he'd drop in on us after he left work. I'll wait here in case he arrives," Donais said.

"That leaves the two of us," Donati said.

As it would turn out, neither would get very far.

CHAPTER 13

P ETRU HAD BEEN hiding for several hours behind a tall bush across the street from Donais's apartment building, and his legs were beginning to cramp from standing in one position for so long. The bush was one of many that were spaced at intervals in front of the six-foot-high brown stucco wall behind him, which went in both directions for as far as the eye could see. In front of the bushes was a sidewalk, and beyond that a line of parked cars.

Finding Bruno and Donati hadn't been hard because Rizzo had written three possible addresses where they might be staying on the back of the photos he'd given him, with the other two locations being the Ritz and Donais's grandmother's apartment. He'd come to this location after calling the hotel and finding that neither Donati nor Bruno was registered there and after seeing that the lights were off at Donais's grandmother's apartment.

Petru was staring at the front door of the apartment building when two men walked out the front entrance. The full moon and the outdoor lighting enabled him to quickly verify that these were the individuals he'd been paid to kill. Removing the gold-plated Beretta from the small of his back, he placed Bruno within its sights. His hands were steady, and his target was walking directly toward him. It would have been an easy kill shot had a person not stepped into his line of sight as he pressed the trigger. The round entered the stranger's back and hurled him forward into Bruno and Donati, sending all three tumbling to the ground as the gunshot echoed throughout the neighborhood. Undeterred, Petru left the cover of the bush and started across the street. As he was moving his gun toward Bruno, who was on his back and fully exposed, he saw Donati dart his hand into the stranger's jacket. A moment later, he was holding a gun, which bucked in his hand as he put two bullets into the asphalt less than a foot to Petru's right. Petru didn't want to challenge Donati's aim a third time and ran down the street with every ounce of energy he could summon, bullets impacting the asphalt around him as he did.

Bruno didn't need a doctor to tell him that St. Amand was dead. The superintendent's eyes were open in a perpetual stare, the bullet having entered his back at a place and angle where it would have penetrated his heart. Not long after the gunshots stopped, Donais ran out the front entrance. She stopped immediately upon seeing St. Amand and dropped to her knees beside him. There was little Bruno could do but watch as she held him in her arms and cried.

"The killer escaped," Donati said, having come back from chasing their would-be assassin. He had lost the man as he weaved through the neighborhood's warren of buildings.

Apparently, a neighbor had called the police because less than five minutes after the first sound of gunfire, officers arrived. An hour after that, St. Amand's body was placed in a body bag and loaded into a vehicle, to be taken to the morgue, while Bruno, Donati, and Donais were told by police to be available for questioning and not leave town.

"I was the target," Bruno said, once they had returned to Donais's apartment. "If he hadn't stepped in front of that bullet, I'd be the one on the way to the morgue."

"You and I were both targets," Donati said, "because Rizzo isn't one to walk away from a grudge—which means that he'll keep sending people after us until we're dead."

"Then I guess we'll have to discover where he's hiding before then. But first we need to find St. Amand's killer," Bruno said.

"Agreed. But how do we do that since we don't even know what he looks like?" Donati asked.

Before Bruno could respond, Donais said, "By going fishing."

"You'll have to explain that," Bruno said.

And she did.

Sometimes finding a parking space on the street in Paris was akin to buying a winning lottery ticket. It could happen, but the odds were significantly against you. So Petru didn't rent a vehicle to go to Donais's grandmother's apartment. There was no telling how far away he'd have to park, especially since it was early morning, and it was unlikely anyone would have vacated their overnight parking space yet. Instead, he took a taxi to within a mile of the address and walked the remaining distance.

Petru knew that Bruno and Donati could still be at Donais's apartment or somewhere other than the three locations he had been given. However, experience had taught him that people didn't tend to go somewhere that was unfamiliar to them and that those who had suffered adversity together tended to stick together. Therefore, if he located Donais, then he'd find his targets. Following that reasoning, he was staking out the grandmother's apartment, at least until the police finished with the area around Donais's residence. If Bruno and Donati didn't show up here by the time the police ended their forensic fieldwork, then he'd return to her apartment building or look into other ways of finding them.

It was eight in the morning when Petru first noticed the area's residents walking down the street below him and getting into their vehicles. He'd selected a good hiding place, using a fire escape to get onto the roof of the building across the street from the apartment house in which Donais's grandmother lived. This gave him an unobstructed view of the front entrance without the possibility of being seen. The gold-plated Beretta was in the small of his back, but he had no intention of using it. Instead, he'd rely on his M82 Barrett .50-caliber rifle. If he'd used it last night, instead of having to get close enough to use the handgun, both targets would be dead.

It was eight thirty when Petru saw Donais pull her vehicle up to the accordion gate. He stood to get a better view as she unlocked the gate and drove her car into the garage, closing and locking the gate behind her before entering the building. Even though Bruno and Donati weren't with her, the assassin believed that they couldn't be far behind.

Bruno and Donati were three hundred yards from the apartment building, having been dropped off by Donais before she proceeded to the garage. Neither believed that St. Amand had been the shooter's intended target, because only the three of them had known that he was coming to Donais's apartment. This wasn't about St. Amand; this was about the satisfaction Rizzo would get from orchestrating their deaths. They also understood that the assassin couldn't let this end unsuccessfully. Someone had hired him to kill them and expected that contract to be honored. Knowing this, Donais had suggested using Bruno and Donati as bait to flush out the killer.

Bruno was the first to see the silhouette at the top of the building across the street from the apartment. He pointed it out to Donati, and the two darted toward the building. Neither was going to make a track team, especially since Bruno, who had only recently quit smoking, had the lung capacity of a gerbil. Donati, who didn't want to leave his partner, kept pace a step behind. Fortunately for them, Newton's third law of motion, which stated that for every action there is an equal and opposite reaction, came into play. When the assassin saw them running toward the building, his primary concern was not getting cornered on the roof. Therefore, he streaked down the fire escape and was running to the street just as Bruno and Donati rounded the corner of the building. The resulting collision sent all three rebounding off one another and sprawling to the ground. When Bruno and Donati looked up, no introduction was necessary. One look at the Corsican, who had a rifle slung over his right shoulder, told them that he was their killer.

Donati leaped off the ground and, lowering his head and shoulder, sprung toward the assassin, who was now on his feet in front of him. The fact that Donati wasn't upright saved his life because the assassin's knife, which he withdrew from his sleeve and flung in the blink of an eye, would have cleaved his forehead if he had been. Donati hit his opponent solidly in the midsection, knocking the wind out of the assassin and himself as both hit the ground hard. Bruno got into the action a moment later, pulling the assassin up and putting him in a headlock to render him unconscious. That was the plan, at least. With Donati still gasping for air and unable to help, what followed happened so fast that Bruno didn't have time to react. The assassin, unable to break the headlock, kicked Bruno in the shin hard enough to make him momentarily loosen his grip. The assassin then removed the gun from the small of his back and spun around. His eyes showed no emotion as he raised the weapon and aimed it center mass. Bruno didn't move because when a professional killer held a gun on an unarmed person, the outcome was preordained— at least that's what he believed. When he heard the gunshot, he looked at his chest and was surprised not to find a hole in him and a smattering of blood. It wasn't until the subsequent sounds of gunfire that he looked at Petru and saw the killer drop to his knees and fall face-first to the ground as the shooter, now standing over him, continued to pelt him with additional bullets, stopping only when she heard the click of an empty magazine. Bruno looked at Donais's face as she stared at Petru's lifeless body and had no doubt that she would have reloaded and put another ten rounds into him if she'd had an additional magazine.

"I'm glad you kept St. Amand's gun for protection," Bruno said. "Are you all right, Lisette?"

Displaying an odd combination of grief and satisfaction, she said that she was.

"I think we know who sent him," Donati said over the sounds of approaching sirens, pointing to the gold-plated Beretta resting on the ground beside the corpse.

Ten gunshots in the middle of a residential area had generated a battery of calls to the police. Having a gun in France was a serious affair, and obtaining one was a complicated process. If Donais had owned the gun with which she'd killed Petru, it would have fallen into Category B of the French gun control laws, which limited ownership to those with a sports shooting license. In addition to a raft of paperwork, this required a gun owner to be an active member of a shooting club, go to the range at least three times a year, and see a doctor once a year who would attest to the owner's physical and mental ability to discharge a firearm. Since Donais didn't have a license to carry a gun, she should have been in a quagmire of trouble. However, all that went away when she showed the responding officers her police officer's badge, which they verified by checking the number engraved on it. Even though her appointment was temporary, she was still one of them, and law enforcement relaxed. Later, when detectives arrived, Donais informed them that the victim was likely the person who had murdered St. Amand and that the weapon beside him was probably the murder weapon. That seemed to shorten their investigation significantly. The fact that Petru had ten holes in his back and had never pointed his gun at Donais didn't change their finding of self-defense.

CHAPTER 14

F RANÇOIS-XAVIER CASTA WAS sixty years old but looked forty. He had thick curly hair that had begun turning from black to gray several years ago and that gave a slightly distinguished look to the athletic sexagenarian, who worked out three hours per day. At five feet nine he was of average height for someone of French lineage, but his thick, muscular torso made him appear overweight and therefore somewhat shorter. His eyes were dark brown, and his skin had the light olive complexion that was so prevalent in the area around Marseille. He might have been considered handsome except for the thick white scar that ran across his right cheek and his misshapen nose, which had been broken more than half a dozen times and had never been properly reset.

He had lived in Marseille his entire life and had never held a job outside the family business. Two years ago, his father died, and he had replaced him as the head of the largest crime syndicate in Marseille. The family he now headed was one of the fifteen families composing the Unione Corse. Casta was notorious for his brutality, but he also had a reputation for honoring his word and scrupulously fulfilling each contract that he accepted. He was therefore furious to learn that Antone Petru had failed. Cesare Rizzo, or whatever he chose to call himself, had always been a good friend of the family and had been responsible for generating tens of millions in profits. Now Casta had the unenviable task of telling this large profit-maker that fulfillment of their contract would take longer than anticipated. Casta was determined to keep this development close to the vest because if it got out that he'd failed to fulfill a contract, it would be an irrefutable sign of weakness to his competitors. He therefore had to kill Bruno and Donati quickly.

Summoning five of his men, he gave them a copy of everything Rizzo had provided Petru, minus the weapon, and sent them to Paris on his aircraft with enough armament to start a small war. They were told they had twenty-four hours to kill Bruno, Donati, and Donais—the last target added because she'd killed a Unione Corse member, and tradition dictated that she needed to die. None of the five asked what would happen if they failed; the answer was obvious.

Bruno, Donati, and Donais had just left police headquarters after giving their written statements about how their would-be assassin had died. Physically and mentally drained, they decided to sit down, get a cup of espresso, and talk about what they were going to do next. Café Madeleine was the first bistro they encountered, and they selected a booth in the corner, where they wouldn't be overheard. After the waiter returned with their drinks, they started their discussion.

"How did Rizzo get mixed up with the Unione Corse?" Donati asked. The police had run the fingerprints from the person Donais had killed and found they belonged to someone named Antone Petru, a member of the Unione Corse from Marseille.

"He probably contracted with them to kill us. They're reputedly deadlier than the Italian mafia," Donais said. "They're not going to stop coming after us until we're dead because their tradition dictates that anyone who kills one of their members also must die. Since we were all part of that altercation, I assume that means they'll target the three of us."

"You're suggesting we leave the country?" Donati asked, looking at Donais.

"That would only postpone the inevitable. What we need is a way for them to cancel the contract without looking weak. The other alternative is to have Rizzo cancel it. That's the only way to stop them from coming after us until, literally, the day we die."

"That's a bundle of joy I hadn't foreseen," Donati said. "How do you know so much about the Unione Corse?"

"Luc told me," Donais said, her lingering sadness still apparent in her voice. "He investigated the murder of someone who was killed ten years after he put a knife into the heart of a Unione Corse member in a bar fight. He moved from Marseille to Paris and tried to get lost in the crowd. That only worked for so long."

Bruno and Donati were quiet for a moment, both wearing somber looks. They empathized with what Donais was going through. After fifteen seconds of awkward silence, Donati changed the subject.

"Any idea where we can stay?" Donati asked. "We obviously can't use your apartment or that of your grandmother—they're too well known."

"I do have an idea," Bruno said.

"Where?" Donais asked

Instead of answering, Bruno stared at her until the place he was thinking about came to her mind.

"They won't be happy."

"Which is why you'll have to give them a call, Officer Donais."

And she did. Though the person who needed to approve the arrangement wasn't thrilled by the idea, he nevertheless reluctantly agreed.

"This is where you both were staying while I was in jail?" Donati asked as he walked through the immense multimillion-dollar condo on the Île Saint-Louis. He apparently was having a hard time believing this was a safe house.

"It's only temporary, and I don't know how long we'll be able to stay here," Donais said. "But at least we'll be safe until we can figure out how to get that contract canceled."

"If we can," Bruno cautioned.

Donais opened a bottle of pinot noir, and they each took a glass out to the patio and sat in the thickly cushioned chairs.

"Putting myself in the place of the family leader of the Unione Corse," Bruno said, "I am sure he feels they have no choice but to fulfill this contract—and quickly. One or more of their assassins is probably looking for us at this very moment."

"Then the cancellation will have to come from Rizzo—letting the Unione Corse off the hook, so to speak. The problem is that we don't know his whereabouts, and even if we did and were able to confront him, why would he cancel it?" Donati asked.

"But if he dies," Donais said, letting these last words linger before continuing, "then we might have room to negotiate a cessation, assuming we have something the Unione Corse wants."

"That's pretty thin," Bruno said. "Not to get ahead of ourselves, but we don't know what country Rizzo's hiding in or what his new identity is. We tried asking the Beirut airport for their manifests, but they not so politely said no. We could ask the Unione Corse, who probably know where Rizzo is hiding because they have contact with him, but they'd kill us before we would get a chance to ask that question."

"It wasn't that long ago that you both were accused of murder and framed so perfectly that neither of you expected to be cleared," Donais said. "Yet you were. Perhaps we should be a little more optimistic."

"We were cleared thanks to Montanari," Bruno said. And at that moment, he could see that all three of them had the same thought.

Indro Montanari was eating a cannoli, not one that came from Rome, which he generally considered to be good but not great, but one that a friend had brought him from Sicily. It tasted exactly like those his grandmother, who was from the small town of Siculiana, had made for him as a child. The shell was perfect—thin, crispy, slightly blistered, with a hint of sweetness, and flared at the end to accommodate more of the sweetened sheep's milk ricotta filling. He tried to pace himself, but he was doing badly. Of the dozen given to him, six were left. He was in the process of decreasing that number when his cell phone chimed. Seeing it was Bruno, he gave the cannoli a reprieve and accepted the call.

Considering what Bruno had requested from him in the past, which on every occasion had required him to break the law, this latest request didn't come as a surprise. Removing the seventh cannoli from the box, he munched on the tasty dessert as he considered how to access the Beirut airport's passenger manifests. The obvious first step, since he didn't read Arabic, was to attach a translation subprogram to his algorithm, which he'd then use to translate the various airline passenger lists that he was going to obtain from the airport's database. Bruno had given him the day that Patric Beaufort and Damien Lowell arrived in Beirut, but not their departure date or the new names they likely used to get to their next destination. However, since Beirut wasn't exactly someplace where one would have an aperitif and enjoy the sunset, at least not without wearing a flak vest and helmet, he expected that Beaufort and Lowell would have wanted to leave the city within twenty-four hours of arrival and that they would have traveled in the first-class cabin, although using another set of names.

Montanari anticipated light traffic at the Beirut–Rafic Hariri International Airport, since the nightly news usually showed something or other blowing up in the city, and normal people didn't like flying into a battlefield. He was therefore surprised to find that the airport was a beehive of activity, averaging 22,465 people per day on 194 flights. If Beaufort and Lowell had indeed left there within a day, then he'd have to search for two people whose names he didn't have and whose destination wasn't known on the manifests of nearly two hundred flights. For that he would need more energy, and he took an eighth cannoli from the box.

Several hours later, down to his last can of Red Bull and with his supply of cannoli exhausted, Montanari threw up his hands in disgust. Although he had managed to hack into the computer system at the Beirut–Rafic Hariri International Airport, all manifest lists for passengers departing within forty-eight hours of the arrival of Patric Beaufort and Damien Lowell had been erased from the airport and airline databases. Rizzo and Voclain were untraceable.

CHAPTER 15

THE FIVE LARGE men with soulless eyes and uncaring faces who stepped off the Air France flight from Marseille to Paris were hardened soldiers in the Casta family of the Unione Corse. They were met at the airport by someone who shared their demeanor and who escorted them to a van in the parking structure, whereupon he handed over the vehicle key and walked away. The five men went into the back of the van, changed, and then drove the vehicle toward their destination, which was in the center of Paris.

Casta had learned from one of his informants that the police and detectives who responded to Petru's murder had come from a police station not far from where he was killed, and they had bagged the gun that Rizzo had given his assassin. The five men had been given this information and were now headed to that station.

The van pulled up to the security gate behind the police building, and the driver inserted an entry card that had been left inside the vehicle. Once the gates parted, he parked his van next to the other police vehicles, and the five men exited. Each carried an automatic weapon and was dressed as a member of the French National Police RAID team.

The five men entered the building and immediately spread out in a predetermined pattern. The officer at the front desk, though confused as to what RAID members were doing in his station, did not appear to be concerned, doubtlessly considering them fellow officers. He never had time to reevaluate that belief because when the RAID member standing before him heard the sound of gunfire coming from the rear of the police facility, he pumped two rounds into the desk officer's chest, causing his body to slam hard against the wall behind him.

It took three minutes to kill the fifteen people working inside the facility and five to find the gold-plated Beretta and return to the van. They then drove to a heavily wooded area forty minutes outside the city, where a minivan was waiting for them. After changing into civilian clothes and swapping vehicles, they returned to Paris.

As expected, word of the police massacre dominated global news headlines. An army of reporters and camera crews crowded in front of the police station where the killings had occurred, hoping to get any information they could from those who entered and left the building. The press was given no reason for the murders because the police knew of none. The only clue they had was the stolen gold-plated Beretta, whose disappearance from the evidence room was not released to the media.

Deputy Police Chief Philipe Valleroy was operationally at the top of the food chain at the Paris police department. He was forty-six years old and was blessed with rugged good looks and a ramrod-straight posture. At six feet two and 220 pounds, the hazel-eyed and prematurely gray-haired officer looked as if he belonged on a police recruitment poster.

Following the massacre and the theft of the gun that had been found on Petru, Valleroy believed that the Unione Corse was to blame. He and the detectives with him drew this conclusion principally because Petru had been a known assassin with the group, and the sophistication of the assault had the earmarks of an organized effort rather than the action of a gang or a few street thugs. However, the seeming incongruity in what had occurred was the theft of the gun. It wasn't until he put that fact together with the statements made by Bruno, Donati, and Donais following the death of Petru that another possibility came to light—the involvement of Cesare Rizzo, alias Gamal Al-Mutairi. Since Rizzo was implicated in the killing of Luc Guimond and another officer, it wasn't much of a stretch to believe that he'd also be involved in the murder of fifteen people to retrieve the weapon that ballistics had shown was used to kill Matthieu St. Amand. There were three people who might be able to explain why the gold-plated Beretta was so important to Rizzo, important enough to risk a worldwide manhunt, and Valleroy was on his way to ask them that very question.

Looking in his rearview mirror as he departed the station, Valleroy saw a minivan pull away from the curb in concert with him and settle into traffic three cars behind his vehicle. The fact that the van left at the same time wasn't in itself suspicious. However, the fact that it maintained its position behind him, even though he switched lanes several times, was. That's when Valleroy decided that he needed an insurance policy.

Thirty minutes after leaving his office, the deputy police chief crossed to the right bank of the River Seine and entered the fourth arrondissement on the Île Saint-Louis. Pulling in front of the building in which the safe house was located, he found no open spaces in sight on the narrow tree-lined street and so parked his police vehicle in a no-parking zone directly in front of the building. His pace was casual and his demeanor calm as he stooped to retie a shoelace and then entered the lobby.

The Unione Corse killers, who were hoping to follow Valleroy to the trio they wished to kill, pulled their vehicle behind the police car. The unofficial leader of the group, which meant the person who had the most kills, directed that they all run after the deputy police chief before he got into an elevator and the door closed behind him. They couldn't allow that to happen. If it did, they'd have to return to their vehicle and wait for Valleroy to leave the building, because there was no way five men carrying automatic weapons were going to be inconspicuous waiting in the lobby. They probably also couldn't get away with leaving their van where it was. Sooner or later, traffic enforcement would come along and direct them to move—after demanding a driver's license to issue a ticket. Whatever the scenario, grabbing a police officer off the street and interrogating him took time, a luxury they didn't have given Casta's order to eliminate their targets within twenty-four hours. So, with no other choice, the men raced toward the building entrance.

Valleroy, whose back was to the entrance, had just pushed the call button and was waiting for the ancient elevator to arrive. Before it did, however, he heard the building door open and someone yell *"poulet,"* the French word for chicken, which was also used to disparagingly refer to a police officer. As Valleroy turned, he saw five men, each holding a FAMAS, a bullpup-style assault rifle capable of firing eleven hundred rounds per minute, all pointed at him.

The clear intent of the Unione Corse assassins was to follow the deputy police chief into the elevator, find their three targets, and kill them along with Valleroy. They'd then get rid of their vehicle and their weapons and take a train back to Marseille. However, they never got that opportunity because at that moment they were surrounded by two French National Police RAID teams. Although the police investigation would later indicate that one of the assassins opened fire first, what happened next was something different. There was no dialogue or call to surrender because each member of the RAID teams had one or more friends who'd been killed at the station house. Each knew without a doubt, because of the weapons that the men before them were carrying, that these were the scumbags who'd killed their fellow officers. The explosive gunfire was one-sided, with the five Unione Corse assassins literally torn to pieces by the ensuing gunfire.

Casta was unaccustomed to failure. He was comfortable being the lion in a valley of lambs, imposing his will on lesser men and ridding himself of competitors who tried to enter his domain. The fact that he'd lost six men didn't bother him; there were always more to take their place. But their failure might make him appear weak, with interlopers believing that he'd become long in the tooth. That perception could be fatal in his line of work. In the past, his response to those who opposed him had always been draconian. After his father died and he took over the family business, there were those who tried to compete with one or more of his businesses, usually drugs and prostitution, by offering product and services at prices well below what he charged. All quickly failed because he'd continued his father's scorched-earth policy of dismembering the bodies of those involved and sending them to their families in a box with a warning that future attempts would result in the dismemberment of their entire bloodline. It didn't take long after that for word to get around and for his monopoly on propagating and profiting from all illegal activities in the Marseille area to reassert itself. Now that fear, which was necessary to maintain his empire, was in danger of dissipating.

Casta wasn't concerned only about competitors; he also needed to maintain the confidence of the other fourteen families that made up the Union Corse. They'd entrusted his family, beginning with his father, with managing the partnership's interests within the port of Marseille. This was the lynchpin of the Union Corse's financial stability and the means by which the partnership made money and yielded its influence. Therefore, in a very real sense, if he had a problem, so did the other fourteen families.

He was certain that the police would link the six men that he'd sent to Paris to the Casta family branch of the Unione Corse. A photo or fingerprint and a few clicks on a police department keyboard would show that they were employed by him and that, on occasion, he'd used them as muscle. Once those dots were connected, the national government would put him—and particularly the port of Marseille—under a microscope. And anything that affected the port affected the partnership. He was caught in the jaws of a closing vice thanks to three people who should, by all rights, be dead.

CHAPTER 16

RIZZO FOUND OUT about Casta's latest failure when he heard the BBC News report that the five men who'd murdered fifteen Paris police officers had been tracked down by law enforcement and killed in an ensuing gunfight. Immediately afterward, he contracted with another group as ruthless as Casta's. Time was on his side because Bruno, Donati, and now also Donais, whom he'd added to this new contract, couldn't evade assassins forever. His only regret was that they wouldn't be killed with his father's gun.

His new country of residence didn't afford him the same lifestyle as Paris, but it was close. He and Voclain had just dined at a three-star Joel Robuchon restaurant and tonight would try a Jean-Georges Vongerichten gastronomical venue. He'd looked at the menu online and was surprised to find Faroe Island salmon, a delicacy that must have been difficult to ship to this area of the world while maintaining its freshness.

Rizzo sat down and poured himself three fingers of Hennessy Beauté du Siécle Grand Champagne cognac from its Baccarat container, then lit a cigar. Tomorrow he would meet the first of several women whom he was interviewing to be his wife. It was time to get married, before he became too old to produce a male heir and teach him the family business. Each of the women in the dossiers had been vetted by a prominent attorney in accordance with selection criteria that Rizzo had provided. He'd viewed their photos and found them equally stunning, all between the ages of twenty and twenty-six. And even though their backgrounds and proclivities were different, they shared one common trait—discretion and an unwillingness to discuss family and friends, one of the conditions he'd established.

He hoped he'd have better luck with creating a family tree than previous generations of Rizzo's. At his age he should have been surrounded by close family and other relatives, instead of being the trunk of a family tree stripped of its branches. He realized that this was a result of three cullings. The first had occurred with the sinking of the steamer SS *Princess Alice* in 1878, when it collided with a collier—a bulk cargo ship carrying coal. The head of the family at the time had rented the vessel for a family reunion in Gravesend, Great Britain. Rizzo's had lived there centuries ago when the area was occupied by Romans, and the family still maintained a castle and significant pasturelands. Unfortunately, the steamer broke in two and sank within four minutes of the collision. Only ten family members, which included the patriarch of the family, were rescued. The second culling occurred with the crash of the *Hindenburg* in 1937. The patriarch, his wife, their children, and other family members had been on board. None survived. The last culling of the Rizzo family had been the most horrific. During World War II, all but two family members had been systematically hunted down and killed by the Nazis, who wanted the family's vast fortune to finance the Reich. Although the Nazis managed to appropriate the family's local real estate holdings, the current patriarch at the time eluded them and escaped to Geneva along with his young wife. The family's wealth had already been sent to Switzerland and dispersed among several banks. The mansion in Bellagio, although confiscated and occupied by the Third Reich, was never bombed and was returned intact after the war. Thus, when Rodolfo Rizzo was born shortly after World War II, he was an only child who later had only one offspring—Cesare.

Cesare Rizzo looked at the $4 million Patek Philippe Observatory chronometer on his left wrist and noted that it was time to leave for dinner. Letting his cigar extinguish itself in the silver ashtray and downing the last of his cognac, he stood from his chair and walked to the elevator.

Valleroy watched the removal of the five bodies from the lobby, followed by the departure of medical and forensic personnel, the RAID team, and other officers who'd secured the premises. He then entered the elevator with Bruno, Donati, and Donais, whom he'd called to see if they could identify any of the bodies. They couldn't.

"I hope the French taxpayer never sees this," Valleroy said as he entered the luxurious condominium. "They wouldn't understand that the opulence of the building makes this an ideal location for a safe house."

"Repossessed from a drug dealer?" Bruno asked.

"How else could we obtain such a place? Even so, the common-area maintenance charges are more than the mortgage and upkeep on my house."

"Aren't the other residents suspicious?" Bruno asked. "A lot of different people must come and go from this residence, and they probably don't look like they have the affluence to buy or rent this condo."

"Most of the residents are either wealthy foreigners or Parisians who travel extensively. Therefore, at most a third of them are in this building at any time. It's doubtful that they'd notice."

All four went onto the patio and took seats at a circular outdoor table on the far left side of the balcony.

Valleroy, who'd been carrying the gold-plated Beretta in his left hand, placed it on the table. "Any idea why five men would kill fifteen police officers to steal this?" he asked.

"Just a theory," Bruno said.

Valleroy spread his hands apart in a gesture that said, "Let's hear it."

"That's the gun Duke Rodolfo Rizzo, Cesare's father, used to kill himself. The trust that purchased his mansion also acquired its assets. I'm guessing that the purchase included that gun," Bruno said.

"And since we believe that Cesare Rizzo is the owner of that trust," Donati continued, "then he easily could have taken possession of the Beretta. It seems that he wants to use the same gun that took his father's life to also take ours."

"He's gone through a lot of trouble and apparently paid quite a bit of money to try to kill the both of you. You realize he's not going to stop until he succeeds?"

"We're painfully aware of that," Donati replied.

"So far, the only thing that Rizzo can be charged with is using a false passport," said Valleroy. "While that's a serious charge, it'll be a bump in the road to someone of his wealth. Given that he'll hire the best attorneys in the country, we'll need something more if we're going to arrest and hold him—that is, if we can even find him. Do you have any idea where he's hiding?"

"Not a clue. We lost him at the Beirut airport after our source told us that the data for every airline in and out of Beirut, along with the airport data on arrivals and departures, was erased for a two-day period," Bruno said. "I'm sure he and Voclain left using another alias."

"So he could be anywhere," Valleroy said.

"That's about the size of it."

Bruno noticed that Donais, who was sitting across from Valleroy, seemed to be lost in thought and not listening to the discussion going on around her.

"What do you think, Lisette?" he said, bringing her back to the present.

"I'm thinking about the Maybach."

"Rizzo's car?" Donati asked.

"Where is it?" she said. "I mean, it's worth at least half a million US dollars. He seems to have taken everything else with him—even the furniture. So why not the Maybach?"

"Perhaps he left it at Le Bourget Airport when he flew to Mayotte," Donati said, "or has it stashed with his furniture."

"Let me check if he left it at the airport," Valleroy said. He hit one of his speed-dial numbers, spoke briefly to the person on the other end, and waited. The wait lasted fifteen minutes, during which time the deputy police chief kept his phone on mute as everyone around the table exchanged small talk. When Valleroy received a response, he thanked the person he was speaking with and hung up.

"The vehicle is not at Le Bourget. The officer I spoke with looked at the digital imagery we have of Rizzo arriving at the airport and boarding the Gulfstream. He arrived in an SUV and not in a Maybach," Valleroy said. "The vehicle could be in storage, along with his furniture, artwork, and anything else he couldn't fit on the plane."

"I believe his furniture and the Maybach are on their way to where he's now living," Donais said. "Rizzo's a narcissist, and his expensive possessions are an extension of that persona."

"I agree with Lisette," Bruno said. "His looks, attitude, and personality are, in many ways, a clone of his father's."

"Let's assume that's true," Valleroy said. "Then it should be fairly easy, given the customs forms that are required, to trace the Maybach and the thousands of pounds of furniture that are probably accompanying it."

"If I know Rizzo, nothing will be easy," Bruno replied.

"It's no secret that the Unione Corse has a significant presence in Marseille," Donais said, "which is also the largest port in France. I don't think it's a stretch of the imagination to say that the Maybach, along with anything else Rizzo wanted to ship to his new residence, probably left from that port. I'd also assume that the paperwork didn't reflect what was being transported."

"And while we've been in Paris dodging assassins, that ship could have already docked or transferred the cargo to another vessel," Donati added. "Moreover, I can't see how we're ever going to obtain the manifests for the weeks surrounding Rizzo's departure, especially since the Unione Corse controls the port. They're not about to turn over documentation that would expose their smuggling."

"Another dead end," Donais said.

"Maybe not," Bruno replied, the expression on his face reflecting confidence. "There just might be a way to trace the Maybach."

"How?" Donais asked.

"By asking the person who knows where it went," Bruno replied.

Bruno explained what he had in mind, and when he was finished laying out his plan, the defensive look on his face indicated that he expected the deputy chief to talk him out of it. But as it turned out, Valleroy liked what he'd heard and volunteered to go with them and smooth out any bureaucratic wrinkles that might crop up. Not wasting any time, they left the condo and got into Valleroy's vehicle for the hour-long ride to Charles de Gaulle Airport.

Departures from Paris to Marseille were frequent, and they were able to board the eighty-minute flight not long after they arrived. Once they deplaned in Marseille and exited the main terminal, they were met by a young police officer holding a sign with Valleroy's name on it. The officer, who was also their driver, told Valleroy that he had graduated from the academy two weeks ago and had been assigned as Valleroy's escort for as long as the deputy chief remained in the city.

Valleroy got into the front seat of the police van and told the driver to head to Aix-en-Provence.

"That's eleven miles from here. It'll take us twenty minutes to get there if we don't encounter much traffic."

As they skirted the Mediterranean and headed out of the second-largest city in France, a working-class enclave of largely blue-collar workers, the huge port of Marseille could be seen in the distance.

"Are you from Marseille?" Valleroy asked the driver.

"I am, sir."

"What can you tell us about the port?"

The academy graduate, seemingly nervous about speaking to someone as senior as Valleroy, cleared his throat and began. "The port and the city are inseparable. Marseille's economy revolves around the port. Hundreds of companies and thousands of families owe their existence and livelihood to the port. Around ninety million tons of goods come across its docks each year."

"You seem pretty sure of that number."

"Most residents can provide that number. The current and historical numbers are always in local articles on the port."

"Do most of the people who work at the port live in the vicinity?"

"Most do," the driver conceded. "But once they become more financially stable, they move to neighboring cities. One such city is where we're headed, Aix-en-Provence. It's a countryside community—you'll see. Interestingly, the largest estate there belongs to François-Xavier Casta, the head of the Unione Corse. I hear that his mansion, which isn't visible from the highway, is massive."

"Is the estate hard to find?" Valleroy asked.

"It's easy. Why do you ask?"

"Because that's where we're going."

The driver, who was a devout Catholic, made a quick sign of the cross. "Sir, that may not be a good idea. Mr. Casta hates the police. Without a warrant, we won't get past the guards at the gate."

"I have a plan," Valleroy replied.

The academy graduate, who'd been talkative until Valleroy gave their destination, didn't say another word until the van approached the entrance to the estate.

The entrance was a large metal gate that spanned a gap in a ten-foot-high white stucco wall, which extended in both directions as far as the eye could see. Parked heel-to-toe in front of the gate were two black Range Rovers, each with two security guards inside.

"It'd take a tank to forcibly enter this estate," Bruno said.

"It's not an estate—it's a fortress," Valleroy corrected.

Bruno's idea, which everyone had agreed to, was to show up at the estate and ask Casta where he had sent the Maybach. Bruno didn't expect him to willingly provide that information, and therefore he was going to use the carrot and stick approach. The stick would be a threat from Valleroy to send the military to supervise all aspects of the port's functions, thereby making it difficult for Casta to conduct his normal business activities of smuggling, drug trafficking, and other illegalities. The carrot was that if Casta provided the information, the military would stay out of the port. The major flaw in this plan, which Valleroy had pointed out, was that there was no guarantee that Casta wouldn't kill them once they left his estate.

Normally a local police chief had zero influence over the military, which was part of the national government. But as Bruno had earlier pointed out when explaining his plan, Casta didn't know what rank or authority Valleroy had. And the idea of the military permeating the port might not resonate well with the other families, who made their money by maintaining a low profile and conducting their illegal activities under the radar of the government. Bruno hypothesized that although this threat might not be enough to trigger a change in family leadership, it would get Casta's attention, since the only retirement home the Unione Corse offered was six feet below the surface.

The police van pulled in front of the two Range Rovers, and everyone but the driver got out. As they approached the vehicles blocking the gate, a stocky man of average height left the lead vehicle. Valleroy handed him his credentials and asked to see Casta.

Probably recognizing that the decision to let Valleroy and his companions into the estate or turn them away was above his pay grade, the man called the mansion. After a brief discussion, he told Valleroy to follow the road to its end, which was five miles away, and someone would escort them to the mansion. The man then motioned for the Range Rovers to move, and once they did, he removed a remote control from his pocket and pressed a button to open the gate. The group continued down the five-mile road, with a thick steel cable fence on either side of the road making it impossible to veer off.

CHAPTER 17

ASTA ENDED THE phone call with the guard at the gate.

"Trouble?" asked his senior security guard, who had served the family for two and a half decades.

"I don't know. The deputy chief of police from Paris is here. That's not unexpected, given that so many of his officers were killed by members of our family. I also won't be surprised if he asks about Rizzo since our men stole his weapon from the police station."

"How would they know who the weapon belonged to?"

"Bruno and Donati have undoubtedly told him."

"I've heard from friends of mine that the other families aren't happy about the publicity from the killings. They won't like the fact that the poulet are here."

"I know. Any issues with the ship?" Casta asked. He wanted to make sure that at least this part of his contract with Rizzo went as planned.

"None that I know," the guard replied.

The ship they were referring to was the *Biruinta*, a Panamanian-flagged freighter out of Marseille that transported goods and people, licit and illicit, for the Unione Corse. Several dozen people at the port of Marseille were on

Casta's payroll, enabling him to alter or create any document or manifest. The Maybach, along with Cesare Rizzo's furniture, had already been loaded onto the *Biruinta* and made it some distance from France the day Guimond attempted to serve Rizzo with a deportation notice. The artwork and other items of value selected by Rizzo had been carefully packaged and transported to one of three Swiss banks.

At that moment, Casta's phone rang, and he was told that his guests were nearing the mansion. Two minutes later, the police van entered the graveled forecourt in front of a four-story thirty-thousand-square-foot French Provencal-style structure, which was surrounded by an enormous expanse of manicured grass dotted with old-growth oak trees. To the right of the mansion were two lighted tennis courts, and to the left was a thirty-meter-long swimming pool surrounded by a large blue-gray slate deck.

Valleroy, Bruno, Donati, and Donais were met by five armed guards. After being frisked for weapons, they were escorted inside while the driver, told by Valleroy to wait with the vehicle, was watched by one of Casta's guards. The interior of the residence was in the Louis XIV style, the furniture inlaid with thin plaques of ebony, copper, mother of pearl, and exotic woods of different colors in elaborate designs. Quickly ushered through the reception area and main salon, they were taken onto the terrace, where they were met by François-Xavier Casta, who had two guards standing directly behind him.

Casta looked at Bruno and Donati. "You've both proved extraordinarily difficult to kill," he said, forgoing all pleasantries and not bothering to hide the fact that he'd been behind the attempts on their lives. He pointed to his right, to a group of thickly padded forest-green outdoor chairs positioned around a rectangular glass table.

"Why are you here?" Casta asked, taking a seat at the head of the table. He pulled a bottle of Pietra, a Corsican beer, from a large ice bucket beside him and told one of his guards to give each of his guests one as well.

After everyone had taken their first sip of the strong chestnut beer, Bruno responded. "We want to negotiate," he said, before taking another swig.

"You have nothing I want, except your lives. It's not personal, but I've accepted a contract to kill the both of you, to which I added your attractive partner, and it would be bad for business if I failed to deliver. You probably know that I can't kill you here because too many people know you're at my estate. But I wouldn't make any commitments beyond this week."

"You misunderstand. We're not negotiating for our lives. We're here to see what you'll give us to protect you," Bruno replied.

Casta, who wore a confused look of incomprehension, stared hard at Bruno. One of the things that he'd bragged about to his senior guard was that he could always spot a liar by their tells. The most common tells were failing to make eye contact, fidgeting, increased blinking, blushing, or turning pale. These physical indicators meant that a person was nervous or uncomfortable with what they were communicating. The biggest giveaway as to their truthfulness, however, was their voice. A change in pitch, use of "mm" or "ah," stammering, clearing one's throat, using humor or sarcasm to change the subject, and being overly defensive were also signs that a person wasn't telling the truth. Casta saw that Bruno didn't display any of these indicators. Therefore, his demeanor changed to one of interest.

"My life is constantly in danger. This," Casta said, touching the long white scar across his cheek, "was given to me courtesy of the French government." He noted the surprise on everyone's faces. "Unfortunately, the agent who gave this to me drowned in a swimming accident not long after. Don't worry about the survival of the wolf."

"Good to know," Valleroy replied, taking the lead on the discussion. "Except the threat isn't from us—it's from the wolf's extended family. The killing of a police superintendent and the slaughter of fifteen police officers has created a public outcry to find and prosecute those behind the massacre. So far, the public is unaware that the men responsible for these murders were members of the Unione Corse, a fact that we've verified by running the fingerprints of the deceased. Once they find out, and after a suggestion from us, I predict that the government will want to appease public anger by ordering the military to take over your organization's purported stronghold—the port of Marseille. How do you think that will go over with the other families?"

Casta didn't answer the question. "What do you want in return?" he asked.

"The whereabouts of Cesare Rizzo and Amo Voclain," Valleroy said.

"Assuming that I provide this information, how do I know that you'll keep the military out of the port?" Casta asked.

"We're not cut from the same cloth. I keep my word," Valleroy replied, causing Casta to flinch in irritation. "If you give us what we want, the story we give to the press will be that the five men killed were after drugs that were stored in an evidence locker. However, they went to the wrong station. They'll be painted as five malcontents from Marseille who were not known to be active members of any criminal organization. No public outcry against the Unione Corse, no port takeover—if we get what we want," Valleroy emphasized.

"I'm going to take a piss. Write this press release, and after I see it, I'll give you my answer." Casta then got up and walked into his mansion while his guards remained on the terrace.

Valleroy took a pen and small notepad from his pocket and within five minutes wrote a press release. When Casta returned, Valleroy handed him what he'd written.

"This is acceptable, if it's released exactly as written."

"I'll need to get the chief of police's approval."

"Then I suggest you call him," Casta said, gesturing for Valleroy to pull out his phone and call his boss.

Removing his phone from his jacket pocket, Valleroy called Jemond Ragon and explained the situation to him. They'd worked together for the past twenty-five years, and the trust between them had been established long ago. Ragon readily gave Valleroy his permission to send out the press release at his discretion once he got what he needed.

Valleroy hung up and confirmed that he had the chief's approval. "Now I believe it's time for you to tell us where Cesare Rizzo and Amo Voclain are hiding," Valleroy said.

"The ship carrying his vehicle and furniture is called the *Biruinta*, named after the city where my late wife was born. I don't have the exact address where Cesare Rizzo and Amo Voclain reside, but if you follow his property when it leaves port at its destination, you'll know."

"And the destination of the *Biruinta*?" Bruno asked.

"The port of Sydney, Australia."

There was a visible sign of relief on the young police officer's face when his four passengers returned to the van, followed by a broad smile when Valleroy asked that they go back to the airport to catch the next flight back to Paris.

"What do you think?" Valleroy asked Bruno once the vehicle was underway.

"I believe the information he gave us is correct. He's smart enough to know that if it isn't, you can issue a second press release indicating that new evidence implicates the Unione Corse. He also understands, or at least I hope he does, that if anything happens to us, the chief of police will issue a corrected press release."

"Then we go to Sydney and meet the ship when it docks," Donati said.

"Can you arrange for the authorities to let us follow the cargo to its destination?" Bruno asked Valleroy.

"I can do that. The Australians have always cooperated with us in the past. But you realize that all we have on Rizzo is a passport violation. We suspect he was involved in the death of Luc Guimond and another officer, but there's not enough proof for a judge to issue an arrest warrant on that charge. Voclain is another matter. Since he shot at you and Donais, I can have a warrant issued for attempted murder. After the attorneys get involved, we have a good chance of eventually getting Voclain extradited to France, but not Rizzo, not for a passport violation."

"I think we should go to Sydney and ruffle some feathers," Donati said. "We can bring the extradition papers with us and, as long as we're there, pay Rizzo and Voclain a visit. Maybe Voclain gives up his boss for a lighter sentence. Stranger things have happened. The worst that happens is that Rizzo realizes we'll keep hounding him until we have the proof necessary to put him behind bars."

"It's worth a try," Valleroy conceded. "It is always better to be proactive than reactive. However, I may have failed to mention that I don't have the funds for your trip. If you go, it'll be at your own expense. Otherwise, my office will have the Ministry of Justice file the paperwork for the extradition of Rizzo and Voclain, and we'll let the process between the attorneys and the courts run its course."

"My credit card will take it," Bruno said.

Donais said that she also was willing to purchase a ticket, unless a certain Milan financier was willing to come up with the necessary funds again.

Donati smiled and said that it would be his pleasure to purchase their tickets, if for no other reason than to see Rizzo's face when the three of them confronted him.

Once they arrived at Charles de Gaulle Airport, Valleroy said his goodbyes and returned to his office while Bruno, Donati, and Donais made their way to the departure area to purchase their tickets. Two hours later, they on their way to Sydney, Australia.

CHAPTER 18

BRUNO, DONATI, AND Donais arrived in Sydney, Australia, at five thirty in the evening, twenty-one hours and fifty-five minutes after they left Charles de Gaulle Airport in Paris. Once they were through customs and immigration, they turned on their cell phones. Bruno had an email from Valleroy notifying him that both the port authority and harbormaster had granted the group permission to accompany customs and immigration officials when they boarded the *Biruinta*, which was scheduled to dock at 9:15 a.m. the following day. He also indicated that the requests for the extradition of Cesare Rizzo and Amo Voclain would be coming, but he was still awaiting approval from the Ministry of Europe and Foreign Affairs.

Dragging after the nearly day-long flight, they checked into the Park Hyatt, cleaning up before going downstairs to the Dining Room, which offered a spectacular view of the Opera House. There they feasted on the day's specials—an appetizer of Sydney rock oysters followed by the main course, Cone Bay barramundi. They ended with a yuzu- and lime-poached fig and a cup of espresso.

In the morning they took a taxi to the building at the port where Valleroy had said they'd be expected, arriving forty-five minutes prior to the *Biruinta*'s docking. They met the harbormaster and a customs and immigration officer, and after introductions were made, everyone took a seat at the conference table in the harbormaster's office. Apparently, Valleroy had discussed the purpose of their visit with the Australian officials, because the *Biruinta*'s electronic manifest was already up on the harbormaster's computer screen.

"Since we have some time," the harbormaster began, "perhaps you'd like me to explain the process of getting goods off a vessel that docks here."

Bruno, Donati, and Donais all agreed in near unison that such an explanation would be appreciated.

"Every ship that arrives in port has electronically sent us a manifest, which is a summation of the bills of lading that have been issued by the carrier for a vessel's voyage. The manifest lists consignor, consignee, origin, destination, number of items, their value, and other information used by customs authorities. I have the *Biruinta*'s up on my computer screen."

Bruno acknowledged that he saw it.

"According to the information Deputy Chief of Police Valleroy provided, what you're looking for is on board. The manifest contains a Mercedes Maybach, along with approximately twenty-two tons of furniture and sundry items, from a consignee in Paris. The delivery address is on New South Head Road, which is approximately nine miles from here," the harbormaster said. He then gave them the exact address.

"How long will it take you to release this shipment?" Donati asked.

"The *Biruinta* is a relatively small freighter, at least compared to those we normally see in port. It shouldn't take more than a day to off-load. Once the required fees are paid, and the shipment is properly inspected and processed into the country, its cargo can leave the port." The harbormaster turned to the customs official sitting beside him and asked, "How long do you estimate that'll take?"

"Five days max."

Bruno stood. "Thank you for your time, gentlemen," he said. "We don't want to interfere any further with your day."

Donati and Donais were not surprised; they knew exactly why Bruno was cutting the meeting short.

"We have the address," Donais said with a smile as soon as they stepped outside. The grins on those standing beside her were equally broad.

"And since there's no need to follow the cargo, I think we should pay Cesare Rizzo a visit," Bruno said as they headed toward a line of cabs along the street outside the main gate.

It wasn't until they entered the neighborhood near the address that they'd been given that Bruno got the look of someone who'd eaten something that didn't agree with him. They were in a commercial area of shops and low-rise office buildings—not the residential area where he had expected the $600,000-plus Maybach to be delivered. Several hundred yards later, Bruno slumped back in his seat and shook his head as the taxi came to a stop in front of the address. Donati and Donais both made remarks that, thankfully, because they were in Italian and French, respectively, were not understood by the taxi driver. They were in front of a Christie's auction house.

They went through the exercise of asking the Christie's manager if they could have the name and address of the seller of the goods that would be arriving from the port. Her refusal was expected, and they left ten minutes after they entered.

Returning to the Park Hyatt, they went into the Living Room restaurant and ordered drinks, even though it was ten in the morning. The server soon returned and handed Bloody Marys to Bruno and Donati and a mimosa to Donais. Once she left, everyone took down a healthy amount of their drink and leaned back in their deeply padded club chairs.

"He was never coming to Australia," Bruno said, the disappointment evident in his voice. "He knew we'd somehow find out where the Maybach and furniture were going and chase them. He's selling whatever he owned, and the money will probably go to an offshore trust. This was another giant waste of our time so that he could get settled in whatever country he's now residing in and cover his tracks."

Donati and Donais looked every bit as pissed as Bruno, and all three finished their drinks without further comment. Donati then held up three fingers to their server, who acknowledged his sign and quickly brought three more beverages.

"Do you think Casta knew he was sending us on a fool's errand?" Donais asked.

"Absolutely," Bruno replied. "He probably had a hard time keeping himself from laughing as he gave us the *Biruinta* and its Australian destination, knowing we'd travel halfway around the world and come up empty. Of course, he'll deny that he knows anything more than he told us."

"We could send out the second press release and make good on our threat," Donais said.

"That's the nuclear option," Donati replied. "Before we do that, let's think of a way that we can extract from Casta where Rizzo and Voclain are hiding."

"Agreed," Bruno said.

Finishing their second round of drinks, they again sat in near silence as each tried to come up with a solution.

"I need something stronger," Donati said. "I don't see our server. I'm going to the bar to get us a drink." With that, he got up and left.

Donati returned ten minutes later with three snifters of Louis XIII cognac. "At three thousand dollars a bottle, it's not exactly Hennessy Beauté du Siécle Grand Champagne cognac, but it will still be quite excellent," he said, passing one snifter to Donais and another to Bruno. "At least we had something go right today. The bartender said the Louis XIII had been on back order, and he just received it yesterday from his distributor. A toast." Donati started to raise his glass, but it got only to chest height before he stopped, the look on his face indicating that his mind was elsewhere. He put his glass back on the table. "Did you ever wonder how hard it must be to get Hennessy Beauté du Siécle Grand Champagne cognac?" Donati said. "Price usually reflects rarity, and three hundred thousand dollars per bottle must mean that there aren't many to be found."

From the looks on their faces, Bruno and Donais understood what he was suggesting. Thirty minutes later, they'd formulated their plan.

It was Donais who came up with the idea. Taking the elevator to the second floor, she went to the hotel's business center, a rectangular room with six cubicles, three to a side, each with a computer and printer. At the front of the room was an information desk and, sitting behind it, an eighteen-year-old geek. The man has shoulder-length blond hair and thick black glasses, and he wore a black T-shirt with the name of some long-forgotten band on it and Levi jeans that had seen better days. His five-foot-six physique was devoid of any noticeable musculature. Donais was there to broker a deal. It took five minutes for the attractive five-foot-four blonde to tell the man what she wanted and negotiate a price. Two hours later, he called and told her that he'd finished.

When Donais returned to the business center, the geek had what he'd created displayed on his computer screen. Once Donais approved it, he gave her a piece of paper with the internet address of the site. In return, she handed him the $400 she'd promised, after which she returned to the bar.

Nothing about Hennessy Beauté du Siécle Grand Champagne cognac was ordinary, which was to be expected if one paid around $300,000 for a 1,000-millileter bottle of the rarest eau-de-vie of Hennessy. The precious liquid was stored in a Baccarat bottle, which itself was presented inside a spectacular chest of melted aluminum and glass, with two glasses on either side of the bottle, each adorned with gold leaf and aluminum. One hundred bottles of this extraordinary, expensive cognac were produced. The average age of those currently in existence was between forty-seven and one hundred years, with the rarest being 150 years old.

Cesare Rizzo, just like his father, was familiar with the best purveyors of fine wine, spirits, and cigars in the world. The merchants who sold him what he needed to indulge these expensive vices constantly attended estate sales and scoured the internet, hoping to convince collectors of the rarest of the rare to part with these hard-to-obtain items. To induce this detachment, the merchants offered princely sums, in the hope of extracting an even greater amount of money from the items' resale. However, Rizzo didn't rely solely on merchants for his supply of these items. The reason was that merchants would sell to anyone for the right price. Therefore, there was no assurance he'd end up with the items he was seeking. As a result, he regularly searched the internet himself for bottles of Hennessy Beauté du Siécle Grand Champagne cognac, not only eliminating the middleman but also guaranteeing that he'd have an unimpeded path to a bottle's purchase if one was offered for sale.

Today as he browsed the internet, his efforts were rewarded. He could hardly believe his good fortune in discovering two eighty-seven-year-old bottles of the rare cognac listed in an estate sale—in a posting made a mere ten minutes ago. With a precariously low three-bottle inventory of the cognac in his wine room, he decided to purchase these before someone else stumbled across them.

His normal procedure for initiating a purchase from his new sanctuary was to contact his offshore bank and have someone there correspond with the seller. Once the merchandise was received, the bank would send it to an associated bank not far from where he was living, after filing the necessary forms and paying the required taxes. The fact that these two bottles were available from an estate and the asking price for each was only $300,000, substantially lower than it should have been considering the age of the spirits, moved him to expedite the purchase—a bargain such as this wouldn't go unnoticed for long. Replying to the seller, he agreed to the price and gave his offshore bank credit card number along with the bank's address as the shipping destination. He then shut off his computer and relaxed.

Donais was surprised at the speed with which Rizzo responded. But her initial elation quickly evaporated when she saw that the shipping destination was a bank in Vanuatu, not a residence. She'd had previous experience with the South Pacific island nation, which relied on financial services as one of the mainstays of its economy. She told Bruno and Donati that noncooperation was a certainty.

"Then we're back to square one," Donati replied, his dejection apparent as he rubbed his forehead and slumped back in his chair.

"Maybe not," Bruno said. "Rizzo is a pampered narcissist. The cognac was only one of the luxuries that he felt he couldn't do without. There are others. For example, what if he isn't willing to part with owning a Mercedes Maybach or Gulfstream G650?"

"That makes sense," Donais said.

"Let's start with the Maybach," Bruno continued. Googling the vehicle, he saw that Rizzo's previous model, the Maybach S600 Pullman, had been replaced by the S650 Pullman, which sold for a base price of around $615,000, with customization features costing extra.

"At that price he could have bought any car," Donais said, "but he chose the Maybach Pullman. He's shown a tendency to stay with what he likes—for example, the cognac. I agree with Mauro. He's very likely to purchase the updated model of this vehicle."

"The same logic could also be applied to the seventy-million-dollar Gulfstream G650," Bruno said.

"Tracking overseas shipments of a Gulfstream and a Maybach won't be easy," Donais added. "Without a court order, they're not going to give us their customers' names and addresses any more than Christie's would. No way."

"Gulfstream is a US company, so it'll be extremely hard to get its customer delivery information," Donati said. "The Americans' privacy laws are, in some ways, more stringent than those in the EU. And from what little I know about Gulfstream G650s, delivery takes a long time. The company my father works for owns one, and it took over a year to receive it after the order was placed."

"We haven't got that long," Bruno said. "That leaves the Maybach, and I believe I have an idea for how we might obtain a list of those who recently requested an S650 Maybach Pullman."

"How?" Donais asked.

And Bruno told them.

CHAPTER 19

P HILIPE VALLEROY LOVED getting to his office early in
the morning before anyone else arrived. He considered
this time a breath of serenity before days that were
typically filled with the stress of preventing and responding
to crime. He was on his second cup of coffee when his cell
phone rang. Looking at the screen, he saw that it was Mauro
Bruno. The conversation between the current and former law
enforcement officers was short and to the point, with Bruno
telling the deputy chief what had occurred in Australia. Bruno
then asked Valleroy if he could get someone at Mercedes to
provide the names and addresses of recent purchasers of their
S650 Maybach Pullman and explained why he believed this
might ultimately lead to Rizzo and Voclain's whereabouts.

Valleroy instantly liked what he'd heard and said that he
thought Bruno was onto something. He agreed that Rizzo's
personality and wealth were such that he wouldn't let himself
be deprived of anything he wanted. Valleroy said that he
knew one person who might have access to this information,
but the person's personality made his cooperation a long shot.
Nevertheless, Valleroy would make the call.

After ending his conversation with Bruno, Valleroy
phoned the deputy police chief of Stuttgart, Germany—a

straight arrow who saw either black or white and seldom gray. They met once or twice a year at European police conferences and had gradually built up a friendship over the course of two decades. Neither had asked the other for any favor during that time. Therefore, Valleroy couldn't predict his response.

Valleroy explained to his counterpart in Stuttgart that he was pursuing the person behind the murder of fifteen police officers in Paris. He then went on to explain that during his investigation, he had received a tip that this person was a recent purchaser of a Mercedes S650 Maybach Pullman, likely using an alias. What he needed was a list of customers who had recently purchased this vehicle.

The response from the deputy police chief of the Stuttgart police department was nearly instantaneous. "You have my full cooperation. However, I may not be able to get this information because the company goes to great lengths to protect the privacy of its customers. Still, I'm friends with several influential people within Mercedes for whom I've done off-the-books favors from time to time. Let me see what I can do."

It was 7:00 p.m., and Valleroy was still chipping away at the paperwork stacked in his inbox when he received a call from Stuttgart. Twelve of these vehicles had been special-ordered since the introduction of the newest Maybach Pullman, with only one purchased in the past month. That order had come from an offshore bank, and therefore the name of the buyer wasn't disclosed. Moreover, Mercedes had received instructions to place this vehicle within a container and transport it to the port of Bremerhaven, where it was to be put aboard the *Drochia*, a Panamanian ship that was reputedly owned by the Unione Corse. The Stuttgart deputy police chief said that the ship's destination was listed as

Marseille, but once it reached port, the container could be transferred and transported anywhere. Valleroy profusely thanked his counterpart and promised to someday return the favor.

It was 2:00 a.m. when Bruno's cell phone rang. The jet lag had finally caught up with him, and he was in a deep sleep during his iPhone's three attempts to get his attention. Finally, the higher-decibel sound of his room phone woke him. Groggy, he answered. Adrenaline started coursing through his body as soon as he heard Valleroy's voice and then kicked into overdrive when Valleroy gave him the information on the Mercedes.

After a shower and shave, Bruno put on his white shirt, blue suit, and light blue tie and made himself a cup of coffee. He sat down on the couch and stared out the large rectangular window at the Sydney Opera House, although he wasn't focusing on the magnificent structure. He'd come to so many dead ends in his search for Rizzo that he was skeptical that he had the information necessary to track him down. But even if he did, then what? Getting Rizzo thrown out of a country for a passport violation wasn't enough, not after what he'd done. Something else needed to be done to bring his victims the justice they deserved, and Bruno thought he knew exactly how to make that happen. Although he'd be breaking the law and risking a long-term jail term, there was no other way to avenge Guimond, St. Amand, Garceau, and the other brave men who had died because of Rizzo's need for revenge—the same sin he'd shortly be guilty of. When Donati and Donais joined him at the Living Room later that morning for breakfast, he would lay out his plan and give them the opportunity to join him. However, if they declined—and he expected that if they had any good sense at all, they would—he was prepared to go it alone. Either way, Rizzo and Voclain were going to die.

When Donati and Donais arrived at the Living Room for breakfast, Bruno was finishing his espresso. With no one especially hungry, they set their menus aside, and everyone ordered an espresso—Bruno's third of the day. Once the server left, Bruno filled them in on his conversation with Valleroy.

"Then there's a good chance that this vehicle belongs to Rizzo. It sounds like the bank purchasing it is the same one that made arrangements to buy his cognac," Donais said.

"And it's going, at least for one leg of its journey, to the port of Marseille. Hopefully, we can track it from there," Donati added.

"Any ideas on how we handle this?" Donais asked, looking back and forth between the two men.

"Before we go there, there's one other thing I want to discuss," Bruno said. "As we've said before, the best we can hope for is to get Rizzo—and Voclain if he's accompanying him—thrown out of whatever country they're in because they're almost certainly going to be using false passports to hide their true identities. I may even be able to get an extradition warrant for Voclain, if he's in a country where's he's extraditable. That's not good enough for me. I'm planning to take a course of action that, if successful, will rid the world of Rizzo and Voclain. But if I fail and survive, I'll probably spend the remainder of my life in jail. I want you to know so there are no secrets between us. Therefore, this may be where we part company."

"Not so fast. What exactly do you have in mind?" Donati asked.

Over the next thirty minutes, Bruno explained his plan. After he finished, it was Donais who spoke first.

"He's responsible for killing the man I'd hoped to marry," Donais said. "I'm in," she said with a tone of finality.

"They killed a great many innocents, including fellow officers and friends," Donati said. "The world will be a much better place without them. I'm also in. And since we're unemployed and don't have to report to work, I suggest we stay here and use this as our base. Judging from our past travels, there's no telling where we'll need to go next."

"You've both shown a remarkable lapse in judgment, but I appreciate you both joining me. Now let's see if we can find Rizzo and Voclain and send both into the fires of hell."

Philipe Valleroy was a widower who lived alone in an apartment not far from his office. He was a light sleeper and awoke after just one ring of his cell phone. As soon as he picked up, Bruno began apologizing for calling at such an early hour. Valleroy interrupted him midsentence by saying that he himself had done just that to Bruno earlier and that it was the reality of communicating from halfway around the world. Bruno then explained his plan, for which Valleroy was the lynchpin. Bruno acknowledged that what he was asking was illegal and could get everyone involved a long jail sentence.

"Do you think?" Valleroy replied. "Mauro, let's be realistic. If we were to leave things as they are now, and you returned to Paris or Italy, then Rizzo and Voclain would probably never be found because my country wouldn't expend the resources to look for someone accused of a passport violation, which happens numerous times a day with all the immigrants coming into France. Therefore, if the sixteen officers who were killed are to get any justice at all, it'll have to come from us. Some people would call this vigilante justice, and they'd be right. Some might call it retribution, and they would also be correct. And although I admit we are a little light on due process, I and the three of you can call what you're proposing rectitude—which is honesty, integrity, and morality all rolled into one word." With a tone of finality, Valleroy concluded, "Now let's get started and fry these two."

When Valleroy entered his office an hour earlier than usual, he started making a list of people he needed to speak with if he was to effectuate Bruno's plan. Five minutes after he'd finished his last call, he saw the chief of police, Jemond Ragon, walk by his office. It was eight in the morning.

The chief was, physically speaking, the opposite of Valleroy. He was five feet, seven inches tall, and looked like a walking fire hydrant, with a stocky frame that might have carried an extra twenty pounds of muscle and with no discernable neck connecting his head to his torso. He was bald and had intense brown eyes and forearms that some compared to Popeye's. The chief had grown up in the ghetto of Mantes-la-Jolie, in the western suburbs of Paris. An only child, he had worked since the age of twelve and had become a police officer simply because he'd grown up living in fear and wanted to help protect others from the wolves. A twenty-seven-year veteran of the force who had graduated from the academy two years ahead of Valleroy, Ragon had been Valleroy's training officer for the year it had taken Valleroy to move from rookie to officer. They had progressed through the ranks in parallel, and most expected that the deputy police chief would eventually occupy the corner office when his mentor retired.

Long ago, they'd agreed that Valleroy would handle operational issues while the chief focused on working with national and local government officials, politicians, and those active in the community. The chief also had responsibility for coordinating budgets and bureaucratic paperwork required of the department. That partnership had worked well over the years, and Valleroy wanted to ensure that bond of trust continued.

Valleroy left his desk and followed the chief down the hall to his office. He entered without knocking and went to the espresso machine on the side counter. He prepared two cups, each a double portion, while Ragon turned on his computer and got ready for his day. Once they were settled on the couch and had taken their first taste of the double espresso, to which neither man added sweetener, Valleroy briefed Ragon on his conversation with the deputy police chief in Stuttgart, Bruno's plan, and the chits he'd called in that morning to implement the plan.

"You know I'll put a stop to this," Valleroy continued, "and reverse everything I've put in motion if you believe I shouldn't go down this road. I'm acutely aware that even though you're not involved in anything I'm doing, and I'll say that I did this behind your back, there will be a substantial blowback if this falls apart. You and I will both be out of a job and will probably lose our pensions, and although there's no doubt I'll be headed to jail, you might follow."

"I'm glad you didn't wait till I came in to get started," Ragon said with all sincerity. "What was it you said to Bruno? Let's fry these two?"

"That was it," Valleroy confirmed.

"Then get it done."

CHAPTER 20

VALLEROY ARRIVED AT Charles de Gaulle Airport at half past nine and got on the ten o'clock flight to Marseille. When he arrived, the same young officer who'd met him during his last visit greeted him outside the terminal and took him to Casta's residence in Aix-en-Provence. The unannounced visit was greeted with the same enthusiasm as before, and Valleroy was again taken to Casta's terrace. This time there was no beer waiting for him, only a look of consternation from someone who was supremely annoyed at this return visit. Valleroy looked at his watch. It was half past noon.

"Is there someplace else you have to be?" Casta asked. "If so, don't let me detain you."

"I'm here because I'm going to make you another deal. However, this time you're going to be more forthcoming about the location of Cesare Rizzo and Amo Voclain, or whatever they call themselves at this moment."

"As I previously said, I have no idea where they are. That hasn't changed. The only thing that Rizzo asked of me was that I transport his Maybach and the contents of the mansion. I told you about the *Biruinta* and traded this information for the press release. Therefore, our business is concluded."

"At this moment the French military is conducting an exercise in the port of Marseille. A few minutes ago, hundreds of soldiers began to arrive from a nearby military installation. They're simulating the retaking of the port from terrorists. Part of this exercise has the military assuming all critical functions at the port until further notice. I'm told that they'll be copying computer and paper records for backup and storage in the event an actual terrorist attack occurs. This exercise has no time limit, and it's possible that training in an environment as complicated as this port could take substantially longer than anticipated."

"Bullshit. The military doesn't initiate an exercise at the snap of a finger. You're bluffing."

"I may have forgotten to mention that I once saved the daughter of the minister of the armed forces. As you might recall, she was kidnapped some years ago."

"That was you?" Casta asked, his expression one of disbelief.

"I hadn't spoken to the minister in years, but just this morning I decided to call and catch up. Did you know that he named his youngest son Philipe? That's my first name, in case you didn't know. And for your information, the military has a long list of exercises or deployments, call them whatever you like, that they can employ at a moment's notice. Terrorists taking over the port of Marseille is near the top of that list. Therefore, the mechanism for getting them here was established long ago."

"If the military was at the port, I would have heard about it." At that moment, as if on cue, his cell phone chimed. As the Unione Corse leader listened to the caller, a sudden redness spread across his face.

"There's more," the deputy chief said, before Casta could speak. "In concert with the army's exercise at the port, the French navy is conducting interdiction drills at sea, searching all ships in the area for possible weapons of mass destruction that terrorists might try to sneak into the country. They decided to start their search with ships named after cities near Biruinta. That's in Moldova. I believe that you named all your ships after cities in the northern part of that country, near where your wife was born. What a strange coincidence."

Casta looked at the contact list on his cell phone, selected an entry, and pressed the number associated with it. The ensuing discussion could only be described as contentious. After Casta ended the call, he didn't speak. But one look at the Unione Corse leader's face told Valleroy that he was struggling to control his anger.

"As I mentioned, I'm here to make a deal. The *Drochia* is carrying a Mercedes S650 Maybach Pullman for Cesare Rizzo." Valleroy held up his hand before Casta, who looked as if he was about to speak, could deny this. "If we search the ship, we'll uncover the car and undoubtedly an altered manifest that will indicate the container in question is supposedly filled with something else."

"Go on," said Casta.

"I don't know if that vehicle will remain on the *Drochia* or be transferred to one or more vessels before it's delivered. You do, but I don't. Right now, that's not important. What I do know is that until I have Rizzo and Voclain in custody—and by that I mean in cuffs—the soldiers and the navy will continue conducting this exercise. I'm sure your extended family will love you for this. Now, where are Rizzo and Voclain hiding, and what names are they using?"

Casta's facial expression indicated that he was considering what options he had, if any. When he didn't reply, Valleroy spoke again.

"As discussed during my last visit, the other families won't be happy that the military is running the port. And if you think they're unhappy about that, wait until they find out that the navy is searching ships at sea. They'll not only confiscate any contraband they find; they'll sell the ships at auction, thereby neutering your smuggling trade."

"What assurance do I have that you'll keep your word?"

"None. But you and I both know you're a dead man if you don't give me what I've asked for. The longer the military stays, the more money you and the other families lose. They'll be pissed at you for dragging them into this mess. Not long after that, I'll be negotiating with your successor to get the information I want. Now give me what I asked for!" Valleroy's tone left no doubt that he'd reached the end of their discussion.

It was over. The look on Casta's face was one of surrender and abdication. He told Valleroy the aliases that Rizzo and Voclain were using, along with where they were hiding.

"Now that we have that out of the way, there's one more thing I need you to do."

When Valleroy told Casta what he wanted, the Corsican shook his head in disbelief. But at this point, to get rid of the military and save his own hide, he'd give Valleroy anything he asked for. Selecting a name and number from his contact list, he relayed what the deputy chief needed and received an acknowledgment that it would be taken care of.

Bruno received the call from Valleroy as he, Donati, and Donais were sitting in the Living Room, having Foster's beers on draft. After listening to what the deputy chief had to say, Bruno gave a thumbs-up sign to Donati and Donais.

"You did an amazing job, getting the French military to put the squeeze on Casta and getting this info on Rizzo and Voclain," said Bruno.

"It was your plan."

"Still, I expected it would take days if not weeks to extract that information from someone as hardened as Casta. You must have been very convincing."

"Casta was angry but also scared," said Valleroy. "I could see it in his eyes. The other families don't want a fight with the government, and if Casta did, they'd hold a retirement ceremony and give him a nine-millimeter send-off, if you get my drift."

"I do," Bruno acknowledged.

"However, I believe we've just become a victim of our own success. Casta wanted to get the military out of Marseille as quickly as possible. Therefore, the container with the Maybach will be the first to be off-loaded from the *Drochia*, after which it'll be trucked to Charles de Gaulle Airport and put on an Air France transport, arriving at Rizzo's new country of residence thirteen hours and four minutes later."

"You've got to be kidding me," Bruno replied, looking at his watch.

"That gives you approximately fifteen hours to get there and meet the contact that I'll arrange to greet you and your team."

Once he ended his call, Bruno updated Donati and Donais.

"Let's see about the airline tickets," Donati said, getting up from the table and going to the concierge desk.

Fifteen minutes later, he returned. "The flight is seven hours and forty-one minutes long, and we leave in ninety minutes."

"The airport's less than ten miles away. We'll make it," Bruno said. "Let's go upstairs and pack."

Forty-five minutes later, they were boarding their aircraft.

Rizzo received the notification from Casta that his Maybach would be arriving by air in less than a day.

"That seems odd," Voclain said after reading the email from Casta.

"It's probably his way of making amends after he botched two assassination attempts on Bruno and Donati. His reputation is worth more than the cost of transport," Rizzo said. "We have thirteen hours. I already have the paperwork from the bank. Call customs and find out what else they'll need to release the vehicle."

Voclain did as he was told, using his laptop to find the number for airport customs. After a brief conversation, he returned to the great room, where Rizzo was smoking a cigar.

"Customs will need several of their forms filled out, which are online and in English, plus the paperwork from the bank proving ownership, your passport—or more correctly that of Patric Beaufort—and the customs fee, paid in cash or by cashier's check." Voclain gave him the amount of the fee.

"Fill out the customs forms while I get the money from the safe."

"We'll need a flatbed truck to transport it to the Mercedes dealership. It needs to be serviced before we can drive it. The official also said that the vehicle was drained of gas prior to being placed in the aircraft, so it will need to be fueled."

"Take care of it."

Voclain gave a slight nod and returned to his computer to fill out the customs forms, after which he'd make the necessary arrangements for the vehicle.

The flight taken by Bruno, Donati, and Donais was late, and they arrived only fifteen minutes prior to the landing of the Airbus A380 carrying Rizzo's Maybach. They were met at their aircraft door by a customs officer and taken to the VIP center, where they were quickly ushered through customs and immigration. Once that process was complete, the official drove them to the cargo customs terminal, where the Maybach would be brought once it was off-loaded, a process that would take approximately an hour.

The cargo customs terminal was rectangular and the size of a football field. Extending diagonally across the right rear corner of the building, forty feet above the floor, was the customs office. That room measured ninety by thirty feet and gave officers a bird's-eye view of the entire terminal. The room was partitioned, with two-thirds open to the public for the processing of documents and the paying of required fees and the other third occupied by eight customs officers. Each monitored a section of the goods below by means of powerful camera feeds displayed on their computer screen.

In the center of the partition was a ten-foot-long, five-foot-high, one-way glass window, to the ceiling. This allowed customs officers in the smaller portion of the room to see what was occurring in the public area next to them.

Rizzo and Voclain arrived at the cargo customs office thirty minutes before the Maybach was brought into the terminal. There Patric Beaufort presented his passport and handed over the required documents and forms, along with a stack of local currency equivalent of $123,000, or 20 percent of the open value of the vehicle. Bruno, Donati, and Donais, along with the customs officer who had escorted them, watched the transaction through the one-way glass.

When the Maybach arrived, Rizzo seemed barely able to contain himself, anxiously pacing the floor while waiting for the vehicle to be removed from the wooden pallet. Once that process was complete, he and Voclain left the customs office and took the elevator to the floor of the terminal. Their timing was perfect because just as they approached the vehicle, the flatbed truck they had hired was backing toward it. For the next five minutes, Rizzo micromanaged the driver on everything from how close he should pull the truck to the vehicle to how he should attach the cable that would pull it onto the flatbed.

"Cesare Rizzo and Amo Voclain!" called someone with an authoritative voice.

Rizzo and Voclain both spun around upon hearing their given names, which were not the ones they'd used to enter the country. Voclain's eyes darted from side to side as he looked for a way to escape. The reason he didn't move was that standing behind the customs officer who'd called out their names were four SWAT police officers in full combat gear. Rizzo, whose eyes were focused straight ahead of him, was not looking at either the SWAT team or the customs officer, but at the three individuals standing behind them—Bruno, Donati, and Donais.

The police officers searched and handcuffed Rizzo and Voclain. As this occurred, the customs officer, now joined by several other customs officials, opened the driver's door of the Maybach and hit the trunk release latch. Apparently knowing exactly where to look, they unlatched and removed the access panel to the spare tire compartment. Inside was sixty pounds of heroin.

CHAPTER 21

I N THEIR BRIEF time in Singapore, Bruno, Donais, and Donati found that the city-country had a majestic garden-like appearance and near-utopian cleanliness. With one of the highest per capita GDPs in the world, it was not uncommon to see a Ferrari parked next to a Lamborghini, which in turn sat next to a Bentley, and so on. There were two reasons for this prosperity in a country of only five and a half million people, they learned. The first was that it had one of the largest shipping ports in the world, which generated a great deal of wealth for a long line of companies and individuals associated with the port. The second was that it was a global financial center—the Wall Street of Asia, so to speak. According to Singaporeans, both areas prospered because of the government's no-nonsense approach to crime.

In most countries there is a presumption of innocence until proven guilty. However, in drug-related matters, Singapore's Misuse of Drugs Act placed the burden of proof squarely on the defendant and not the government. Accordingly, if a person was caught with a large quantity of drugs, then there was an automatic presumption by the government that the person was trafficking. If the person failed to convince the court otherwise, there was a singular punishment for such a crime: death. According to the law, ignorance was not a defense. If someone owned a house or a car in which drugs were discovered, the law presumed that the owner had possession of the drugs, unless they could convince the government otherwise. Again, the burden of proof was on the defendant. In the case of heroin, a person was presumed to be a trafficker if he was caught with greater than two grams. In Rizzo's case, the drugs hidden in the spare tire compartment of the Maybach amounted to 27,216 grams.

Rizzo and Voclain were taken directly from the airport to the Changi Prison complex in the eastern part of the city. Since they were accused of a capital offense for which the punishment was death, there would be no bail. That was unfortunate because as clean and spacious as the country was, its jails were the antithesis. The cell that Rizzo and Voclain were thrown into had forty sleeping mats and one toilet, which was odorous and not well maintained. And since the other prison inmates had long ago established their own pecking order, newcomers were always given the sleeping spaces closest to the toilet.

The Air France flight from Singapore to Paris took thirteen and a half hours. Upon landing, Bruno, Donati, and Donais went to Donais's apartment and were soon joined there by Valleroy, who brought a bottle of Veuve Clicquot champagne in celebration of their apprehension of Rizzo and Voclain. None of the three had elected to go to the Changi Prison before departing Singapore. Now that Rizzo and Voclain were in custody for a capital offense, the group was content to let Singapore balance the scales of justice for them.

"A toast," Valleroy said, lifting his glass. "To chief inspectors Bruno and Donati and to an amazing investigator,

Lisette Donais. Although only a few select individuals will ever know what you've done to bring justice to our fallen officers, you will forever be held in the highest esteem by those of us who do."

"And to you, Deputy Chief Valleroy," Bruno said. "Without you convincing Casta to place the drugs in the trunk of the Maybach, and obtaining the cooperation of the military, our efforts would have proved fruitless."

Everyone drank, and Valleroy was in the process of pouring a second round when Bruno approached him.

"I'd like to make one slight correction to your toast," Bruno said.

"Oh?"

"We're no longer chief inspectors. A more accurate description would be former chief inspectors, unemployed former law enforcement officers, or McDonald's applicants," Bruno teased.

Valleroy laughed, held up a finger, and set the bottle down. "I might have forgotten to mention that I received a phone call while you were in transit. It seems that you both have been reinstated. Once the head of your state police received a copy of the report issued by Claudine Noel and discovered that you'd been framed, he was quick to offer reinstatement. And as far as you're concerned"—Valleroy turned toward Donais—"the badge you're carrying is now permanent, Lieutenant Donais. You'll have to go to the academy as a formality, but your rank and badge will be waiting for you upon graduation."

While Valleroy spoke further with Donais, Bruno turned to Donati. "It looks as if you'll once again be terrorizing the criminal elements in Milan," Bruno said.

Donati smiled, on the surface seeming to look forward to his return to police work. But Bruno suspected there was something behind his friend's lack of response. It was time to put his own cards on the table.

"Elia, I won't be returning to my chief inspector duties. I'm leaving the state police and forming a detective agency. I've been thinking about this ever since we brought down the patriarch. I enjoy working outside the system, where I'm unconstrained by politics, superiors, or the need for political correctness. I can't go back."

Donati stared at Bruno for a few seconds before responding. "That doesn't work for me unless I'm your partner."

"Come again?"

"I could return to my former job, but just like you, I've thought about my future. After bringing down the patriarch and now his scion, I've acquired a taste for independent investigative work. You've given me the perfect excuse to leave. Milan will do fine without me, Mauro."

"Are you two trying to exclude me?" asked Donais, who had been listening to their exchange along with Valleroy, who stood beside her. "How about a threesome, so to speak? If you'll have me."

"What about going to the academy?" Donati asked.

"She already turned it down," Valleroy said. "She loves being an investigator more than the idea of becoming a police officer."

"And what about you?" Bruno asked Valleroy. "Care to join the three of us?"

"As tempting as that is, considering the extraordinary salary the French government pays me, I'll have to turn it down. The police chief is a close friend, and he needs me.

Until he retires, I'm here. Besides, the three of you will need a good friend inside the department."

"To friendship then," Bruno said, picking up his glass and raising it in a toast.

Later, they walked to a nearby bistro, where the four celebrated that friendship with food and a good deal of wine.

As Bruno, Donati, and Donais were landing in Paris, the fourteen other families that composed the Unione Corse were voting to rid themselves of a liability that affected each of them. They dispatched their chief problem solver, who later that day breached Casta's perimeter security and climbed an olive tree five hundred yards from the mansion's patio. His target was, as usual, seated outside. After gauging the wind and making the proper adjustment to the sight on his rifle, the assassin put his target within his crosshairs and slowly squeezed the trigger. The heavy round hit Casta in the back of the head and exited with such force that his face was blown away. Ten minutes later, his successor, twenty years his junior, walked onto the patio. Casta's security team, who understood that their oath was to the Unione Corse and not an individual and that any deviation from that belief would give them the same retirement option as their boss, placed Casta on a plastic tarp, rolled it up, and carried the body to the waiting Range Rover.

Once the Singaporean government learned that Rizzo and Voclain were Italian citizens, they arranged for an embassy official to meet with the prisoners. However, with the pair's fake passports and the trunk full of heroin, there was nothing the Italian official could do. The trial, therefore, went as predicted. Both Rizzo and Voclain were sentenced to death by hanging, with imposition of the sentence suspended for a short period of time by an appeal, which went nowhere. At dawn on a Friday, the traditional time for hanging at the Changi Prison, both were led to the long-drop gallows. Their hands were bound behind their backs and their legs secured together before the executioner placed black hoods over their heads and fastened the nooses around their necks. Without a word the sentence of the court was then carried out. Moments later, after a doctor pronounced them dead, they were placed into separate cardboard coffins and taken to the crematory, after which their ashes were thrown on the barren patch of ground behind the prison and left to scatter into the wind.

AUTHOR'S NOTE

This is a work of fiction, and the people, institutions, and companies described and everything else mentioned within are not meant to depict anyone or any circumstance in the real world.

Part of the fun in writing novels is immersing the reader in places that the author has visited and, in some instances, formed an emotional attachment to. One such place for this author is the Ritz Paris, which is in a class by itself in the world of hospitality. Therefore, my profuse apology to ownership and management for littering your hotel with bodies and minimizing your camera security system. From experience, the author knows that hotel security is unobtrusive and first-rate. In addition, although the description of the exterior and interior of the hotel is accurate, the author took liberties, for the sake of the storyline, in describing the camera system, the monitors, and just about everything else to do with the hotel's visual and physical security. The photos on the author's website, alanrefkin.com, were taken at the Ritz Paris by Gaetan Lescuyer, one of the most renowned and amazing photographers in the world.

La Santé Prison, which means "prison of the health," exists and has both a VIP and a high-security wing. It is one of three prisons in Paris and is located east of the Montparnasse district in the fourth arrondissement. One of its most notable prisoners was Manuel Noriega, the Panamanian dictator, who was imprisoned there from 2010 to 2011 for money laundering. He was later extradited to Panama.

The École Normale Supérieure, or ENS, is one of the most prestigious institutions of higher learning in France. The school is small, recruiting just two hundred core students, half in the sciences and half in humanities, each year. The description of the school and its location in the fifth arrondissement is accurate, although the author took liberties in the description of the buildings, the layout, and the curriculum for the sake of the storyline.

My thanks to James Marshall, who worked at Starbucks, for the recipe used by Bruno to keep the energetic waiter busy and away from Lisette Donais. It was, as Luc Guimond noted, extraordinary.

The explanation given by Montanari to Bruno regarding how to tell if a digital image or video stream has been altered is accurate. My thanks to Belinda Smith, science reporter for ABC Science, for her article "Fake News, Hoax Images: How to Spot a Digitally Altered Photo from the Real Deal." It provided a detailed yet easy-to-understand explanation of how to detect fake digital imagery.

The Île Saint-Louis is one of two natural islands in the Seine, along with the Île de la Cité, and is connected to both banks of the river by four bridges. It is as represented—a quiet district with condos costing up to $4 million. Entering it is akin to stepping into a time machine that takes you back to the seventeenth- and eighteenth-century neighborhoods of Paris.

Deportation from France is a defined legal process with which the author took liberties. Four years short of a law degree, the author abbreviated the process for the sake of the storyline and to start Rizzo and Voclain on their journey.

Thank you to my niece, Kelsey McGough, for her input and insights into the obfuscation used by the Gulfstream G650 in leaving Le Bourget for Mayotte. The guidance on VFR and IFR restrictions, provided by the star controller working air traffic control in Des Moines, Iowa, was greatly appreciated.

Gun laws in France are very strict and are as described. There is no right to bear arms in that country, and to procure a firearm, you need a hunting or sporting license, which requires a psychological evaluation. If you have any criminal record, you're automatically denied. France is the biggest hunting country in Europe, and most of the gun ownership there is by hunters.

The Unione Corse is as described—a criminal organization primarily concentrated in Corsica and Marseille. Similar to the mafia, it's split into separate crime families. The Unione Corse were the primary organizers of the French Connection and had a virtual monopoly on the heroin trade between France and the United States between the 1950s and 1970s.

Indro Montanari's description of his Sicilian cannoli came from the author's recollection of those made by his grandmother, Anna Bruno, who was from the small Sicilian town of Siculiana. Knowing that memories are always imperfect, the author still believes that no better cannoli has ever been made.

The information presented on the Beirut–Rafic Hariri International Airport is correct. In 2018 it handled over 8.2 million passengers and 71,169 flights. That translates into civilian traffic of approximately 22,465 people per day, arriving on 194 flights—a degree of air traffic that was unexpected by this author prior to his research.

Marseille is the second-largest city in France after Paris. Its commercial port is the largest in the country and processes one hundred million tons of freight per year. Some forty-five thousand jobs are associated with port activities, adding four billion euros to the regional economy. For the sake of the storyline, the Unione Corse was described here as essentially controlling the port of Marseille. However, although the organization has a significant presence in Marseille, the extent of its involvement with the port is unknown.

Aix-en-Provence is accurately described and is located north of Marseille in the foothills of the Alps. The countryside surrounding the city is gorgeous, with carpets of lavender interspersed among the vineyards and orchards. In the distance one can view the Sainte Victoire and its white limestone cliffs. Famous for its outdoor markets and beautiful pedestrian lanes, it's the hometown of Paul Cézanne and Émile Zola. When you're there, try the Les Deux Garcons café, which was frequented by Cézanne.

The Park Hyatt Sydney is a wonderful hotel, nestled under the Harbour Bridge and across from the Sydney Opera House. It is as described, and the dinner items ordered by Bruno, Donati, and Donais were taken from the Dining Room menu.

The Mercedes S650 Maybach Pullman is as described. At twenty-one feet long, it is four feet longer than the regular S-Class Mercedes and twenty-plus inches longer than the longest Rolls-Royce. The passenger seats are forward-facing business jet–style reclining seats, and between compartments, there is an electronically controlled glass partition that turns opaque at the touch of a button. Its base price is, as stated, $615,000.

The Gulfstream G650 is as depicted. It's a top-of-the-line business jet with a range of over eight thousand miles, enabling it to go from London to Los Angeles. The aircraft can attain a speed of Mach 0.95, nearly the speed of sound. Its price tag varies, depending on the customization desired, but it's in the $70 million range.

The information regarding Singapore, a city-state and island country at the southern tip of the Malay Peninsula, is accurate. It is one of the most beautiful countries the author has ever been to. It is often referred to as the Garden City because of the extensive greenery and cleanliness of the island. When you're there, go to the Marina Bay Sands, a $5.5 billion hotel, casino, shopping, and restaurant complex on the bay, and Gardens by the Bay, with its Supertree structures and skywalks overlooking the gardens. If you're adventurous, go to the most famous hawker, or street food, stand in the world: Hong Kong Soya Sauce Chicken Rice and Noodle, which was awarded a Michelin star. That's correct—a food stand received this prestigious award! When you go, make sure it's to the original stand in the large food court (not all that easy to find, but locals will give you directions) and not the follow-on site that's air-conditioned. The author had a phenomenal chicken and rice meal for $3, although there are other items on the limited menu. Be prepared to wait—the author and his wife were in line for an hour, which Singaporeans report is half the average waiting time. The day the author was there, a famous chef who has a Michelin three-star restaurant in New York was waiting in line behind him.

The author made up his own rules for the customs procedures in Singapore, for the sake of the storyline. Mea culpa. The author does extensive research to try to ensure that details in his novels are accurate within the confines of the storyline, but the Singaporean customs agency doesn't like disclosing all that much information, and they didn't seem wild about giving a tour of the facility.

Singaporean drug laws are draconian, and the penalties for violating them are accurately described. The Misuse of Drugs Act creates the presumption that one is trafficking, even for threshold amounts of drugs. The burden for disproving this presumption lies squarely with the defendant and not the government. The penalty is almost always death. The law even presumes that one is in possession of drugs if that person has the keys to a vehicle, structure, home, or other entity that contains drugs. There is also a presumption that if you're in one of these locations, you've been smoking or administering a controlled substance. Therefore, although the author is not an attorney, his understanding is that if you're in the company of users, you're assumed to also be one. Again, the presumption is guilt, and the defendant has the burden to convince the government and courts otherwise— the opposite of what it would be in a US court of law.

Changi Prison is in the eastern part of Singapore and houses the country's most serious criminal offenders, including those sentenced to death. As indicated, execution in Singapore is by hanging, with the sentence traditionally carried out on a Friday morning.

The Scion came about as a natural continuation of *The Patriarch*. The fact is, the end of that novel provided such a cliff-hanger that the author couldn't stop writing. Both the Mauro Bruno and Elia Donati characters gave the author so much to work with that having them start their own agency, with superstar investigator Lisette Donais, seemed to be a great way to initiate future adventures.

ACKNOWLEDGMENTS

As mentioned in previous novels, the author has an amazing group of friends who have unselfishly contributed their technical expertise and provided their feedback throughout the writing process.

To Kerry Refkin for her editing expertise and character profiling. Thank you for standing behind the curtain and providing your extraordinary expertise.

My continued thanks to this group for their valuable insights: Scott Cray, Dr. Charles and Aprille Pappas, Dr. John and Cindy Cancelliere, Kelsey McGough, Doug Ballinger, Alexandra Parra, Mark Iwinski, Mike Calbot, Dr. Meir Daller, Ed Houck, and Cheryl Rinell.

Thank you to Zhang Jingjie for her always extraordinary research and fact-checking.

Thank you to Dr. Kevin Hunter and Rob Durst for taking time away from their technology company and consulting with the author on computer programming, cybersecurity, and IT.

To Clay Parker, Jim Bonaquist, and Greg Urbancic: thank you for the extraordinary legal advice you provide.

To Bill Wiltshire and Debbie Layport: thanks again for your superb financial and accounting skills.

To our friends Zoran Avramoski, Piotr Cretu, Aleksandar Toporovski, Neti Gaxholli, and Billy DeArmond: thanks for your insights.

To Winnie and Doug Ballinger and Scott and Betty Cray: continued thanks for all you do for the countless people who are unable to help themselves.

ABOUT THE AUTHOR

Alan Refkin is the author of five previous works of fiction and the coauthor of four business books on China. He received the Editor's Choice Award for *The Wild, Wild East* and for *Piercing the Great Wall of Corporate China*. The author and his wife, Kerry, live in southwest Florida, where he is currently working on his next Bruno-Donati-Donais novel. More information on the author, including his blog, can be found at alanrefkin.com.

Printed in the United States
By Bookmasters